Saving lives in St. Victoria!

Welcome to paradise! Or, as it's officially known,
the Caribbean island of St. Victoria—
home to chief of staff Nate Edwards and his private
hospital, The Island Clinic. With the motto
"We are *always* here to help," The Island Clinic
was created as both a safe haven for the
rich and famous to receive medical treatment
and a lifeline for the local community.

This summer, we're going to meet
The Island Clinic's medical team as they work hard
to save lives…and, just maybe, get a shot at love!

How to Win the Surgeon's Heart
by Tina Beckett

Caribbean Paradise, Miracle Family
by Julie Danvers

Available now!

The Princess and the Pediatrician
by Annie O'Neil

Reunited with His Long-Lost Nurse
by Charlotte Hawkes

Coming soon!

Dear Reader,

Writing is easiest for me when it's personal. And even though I didn't come up with the idea for The Island Clinic—a medical center in the Caribbean that treats the rich and famous—this might be my most personal book yet.

Willow Thompson, nurse and single mom, has always longed for the love of a family. My own mother was single for a few years when I was the same age as Willow's daughter, Maisie, and Willow's struggles are drawn from the challenges my mother faced.

Of course, Willow has some difficulties that my mother never mentioned. Including a mix-up at the fertility clinic that resulted in using the wrong man's sperm for her pregnancy. Four years later, Willow is shocked when that same man arrives on her doorstep, introducing himself as Maisie's father. His tousled hair and kissable lips are hard to resist, but she does her best—until he gets a job working alongside her.

Willow's been through some betrayal, and she's not sure she's ready to open her heart again. But if she can, she might find the family she's always dreamed of.

Enjoy your visit to The Island Clinic!

Warmly,

Julie Danvers

CARIBBEAN PARADISE, MIRACLE FAMILY

———

JULIE DANVERS

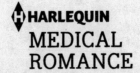

HARLEQUIN
MEDICAL
ROMANCE

Special thanks and acknowledgment are given to Julie Danvers
for her contribution to The Island Clinic miniseries.

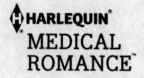

HARLEQUIN®
MEDICAL
ROMANCE™

Recycling programs
for this product may
not exist in your area.

ISBN-13: 978-1-335-40864-8

Caribbean Paradise, Miracle Family

Copyright © 2021 by Harlequin Books S.A.

This edition published by arrangement with Harlequin Books S.A.

For questions and comments about the quality of this book,
please contact us at CustomerService@Harlequin.com.

Harlequin Enterprises ULC
22 Adelaide St. West, 40th Floor
Toronto, Ontario M5H 4E3, Canada
www.Harlequin.com

Printed in U.S.A.

Julie Danvers grew up in a rural community surrounded by farmland. Although her town was small, it offered plenty of scope for imagination, as well as an excellent library. Books allowed Julie to have many adventures from her own home, and her love affair with reading has never ended. She loves to write about heroes and heroines who are adventurous, passionate about a cause, and looking for the best in themselves and others. Julie's website is juliedanvers.wordpress.com.

Books by Julie Danvers

Harlequin Medical Romance

From Hawaii to Forever
Falling Again in El Salvador

Visit the Author Profile page at Harlequin.com.

To Charlotte, who always sees the potential.

CHAPTER ONE

"COME ON, MAISIE! Kick! You can do it!"

Willow Thompson clung to her three-year-old daughter's chubby little hands as Maisie did her best to keep herself afloat in the shallow water. The beach behind their home on the island of St. Victoria was an ideal place to learn to swim, as the water curved into a sandy cove that provided refuge from the strong waves of the Caribbean Sea.

Willow could have chosen to live at the accommodations provided by her workplace. She was a nurse at the Island Clinic, a private clinic in the Caribbean that specialized in providing top-notch medical care to some of the wealthiest and most well-known patients on earth. The clinic prided itself on its ability to provide patients with luxury almost as much as its ability to provide quality health care, and the clinic's extravagance extended to its staff quarters.

But as much as Willow enjoyed elegance,

she enjoyed balance between her work and personal life even more. The small cottage she'd rented on the beach offered privacy for herself and her daughter, and gave Willow the separation from work that she needed. As much as she loved her job as a nurse, part of the reason she'd taken the job was so that she could put work behind her at the end of each day and focus on spending time with her daughter. And living apart from the clinic gave Willow the chance to fully immerse herself—and Maisie—into island life. Willow wanted her daughter to take advantage of all that growing up in the Caribbean had to offer. Which, at the moment, included swimming lessons.

Most island children learned to swim almost before they could walk, but Willow and Maisie had only moved to St. Victoria in the past year. As Maisie paddled in the gentle waves, Willow thought, for what felt like the hundredth time, of how right she'd been to move from their dreary North London flat to the sun-drenched Caribbean islands. In London, swimming lessons would have been impossible on Willow's budget. In fact, just about everything in London was a strain on her budget. Between her modest income as a critical care nurse, and the small amount of money her grandmother had left in trust for Maisie before she passed, there was never much left over after accounting for rent and childcare.

Willow had lived her whole life in Islington, raised by her grandmother. Though they didn't have much, she'd never once felt poor, because Gran had always made her feel loved. But becoming a single mother had opened Willow's eyes to just how wide the divide was between the haves and have-nots. She constantly had to deny Maisie all the little "extras" that her preschool classmates were able to enjoy. Worse, after working all day, Willow only had time to spend a few exhausted hours with Maisie each night. She'd ached to have a child for so long, but felt as though Maisie's childhood was passing her by. The final straw came when she'd picked Maisie up from day care and learned that her daughter had spoken her first word. Willow was devastated that she hadn't been there to hear it. That very night, she decided that she and Maisie needed a change. She hadn't been certain, at first, of what that change would be, but she knew that it needed to be as different from North London as possible.

St. Victoria certainly fit the bill. The vast turquoise waters and boundless blue sky of the island were a stark contrast to London's relentless clouds and smoke. Their little house on the beach was small, but cozy. Like many homes in the Caribbean, it was raised on stilts to protect against flooding and hurricanes. The back door opened directly onto the beach, which was a toddler's delight. There was plenty of sand for Maisie to play in, a network of tide pools to explore and miles of clear, gentle water, perfect for swimming.

Of course, one would have to learn how to swim first. Maisie furrowed her brow in concentration as she kicked her legs in the water.

Living on the beach as they did, Willow had known that she'd need to teach Maisie to swim as quickly as possible. But they'd hit a snag almost as soon as they'd started: Maisie was unwilling to submerge her head under the waves. She could kick her legs, but she refused to put her face into the water. As Maisie began to huff and puff, Willow stood her daughter up in the waist-high water.

"Look, darling. You must put your face into the water if you are to learn to swim."

"Don't want to." Maisie's lower lip began to pout, an expression Willow knew all too well.

"Mummy can do it. See?" Willow quickly dunked her own head under the water and then broke the surface. "It's not hard. It feels lovely."

Maisie's lower lip began to tremble, and Willow knew that tears were likely to come next. Maisie was usually a very agreeable child, rarely protesting against Willow unless she felt anxious or in need of reassurance. So far, tantrums were a rare event in their little two-person household by the sea. But Willow knew that once the tears started coming, there would be no closing the floodgates again until Maisie had had a good cry. What had started as a pleasant day could turn to tears and storm clouds if Willow pushed Maisie before she was ready.

Perhaps they'd had enough of the sea for one day. Willow wanted swimming to remain a fun experience for Maisie, so the girl would feel confident in the water. Pushing Maisie any further today might spoil it.

"All right, then. Maybe that's enough swimming for this morning. Run up to the house and get your sand toys. Show me what kind of castle you can build on the beach."

Maisie's face broke into a smile, and she sprinted ahead of Willow onto the beach.

As always, it brought Willow joy to see Maisie happy. But she also felt a pang of uncertainty that was becoming all too familiar as Maisie grew. Had she done the right thing, giving in so easily when Maisie didn't want to put her head under the water? She never wanted Maisie to feel pushed to do anything she was afraid of. But on the other hand, children needed to be challenged. If she always gave in at the first sign of Maisie's lip trembling, wouldn't that create its own set of problems later on? Willow wanted her daughter to be resilient. If she was too soft on Maisie, her daughter might begin to think she could avoid anything unpleasant simply by crying.

Oh, who am I kidding, she thought. *Maisie's already got me wrapped around her little finger, and she probably knows it.*

Willow wondered if her fate, as a single mother, would involve forever questioning whether she was pushing Maisie too hard, or not enough. Although she had never regretted her decision to raise Maisie on her own, one of the hardest parts about single parenting had been learning to trust her instincts. Her grandmother had passed away shortly after Maisie was born, and Willow had no other family she could ask for advice. At times like this, when she found herself questioning whether she'd given in too easily, she longed for someone who could offer support. Someone she could trust, and who she could rely on to watch over both her and Maisie.

It was a nice dream, but Willow was a practical person. Any dreams of a partner for herself, or a father for Maisie, were unlikely to ever become more than dreams.

She'd always wanted to have children. As a nurse, she'd had so many chances to see first-hand the joy that new babies brought to their parents. Moreover, she'd seen the support that families brought to one another when going through hard times. But Willow had always felt like an outsider as she watched families comfort one another through hardships. At home, it was only herself and Gran. But when Gran had passed away, there had been no one to comfort Willow.

Growing up with Gran had felt special, because it was just the two of them, but it had also felt lonely at times. Willow had always wondered what it would be like to grow up in a large family, with siblings and cousins to share joys and sorrows. Since she couldn't change her own childhood, she decided that she would do the next best thing by having plenty of children of her own. For many years, she'd dreamed of starting a family, and she'd always thought that Jamie, her childhood sweetheart, was dreaming along with her.

Jamie had always agreed that he, too, wanted to get married and have a big family—but he wanted to wait for the right time to start. For eight years, Willow waited with him. She waited as Jamie went through career changes, as he started and dropped out of educational programs and as she watched many of her friends get married and start families of their own. Finally, after her best friend's wedding, she decided she'd waited long enough. She confronted Jamie and asked exactly when they were going to get married.

"What's the rush?" he'd asked. "We've got all the time in the world for that sort of thing."

But Willow knew that wasn't true. As a nurse, she knew that a mother's age had an impact on an infant's health, and newer research was showing that the age of the father had an impact, as well. Even though she'd seen plenty of women give birth to healthy babies well into their forties, she wanted to avoid any increased risk. If she and Jamie were going to have children, she wanted to start soon.

That was when Jamie had dropped his bombshell. He didn't want children. *Any* children. He'd never really been interested in starting a family at all. And when she'd asked him why he'd never shared this rather important information with her, his easy explanation left her breathless.

"You've been talking about having children for years," he'd said. "How was I supposed to tell you that I realized that I didn't want kids?

I thought you'd break up with me if you knew the truth. It just seemed easier not to say anything until it was too late. You can't blame me for keeping quiet. I was just trying to keep us together."

His explanation made things so much worse. Jamie hadn't just changed his mind about wanting children. He'd *never* wanted children, and for years he'd told her otherwise because it was what he'd thought she wanted to hear. She felt as though her dream of having a large family was slipping though her fingers, but worst of all, she felt manipulated and betrayed.

After the breakup, she'd despaired of ever having a child. She'd never dated much before Jamie. He'd been her first serious relationship. And now, after eight years with one person, she felt clumsy and awkward on the dating scene. It didn't help that her trust in men—and in herself—felt irreparably shattered. She was certain she would never be able to trust anyone enough to be in a relationship again.

But even though she was done with relationships, she wasn't done with her dream of having a family. She couldn't be. Her heart ached to even think of it.

And so she'd decided to take a different path. If there was one thing Gran had taught Willow, it was to not let obstacles stop her.

There were many ways to have a family, and Willow wasn't going to let one broken dream get in the way of another.

Gran had wholeheartedly approved of Willow's decision to have a child via donor insemination. Willow was unfazed by the idea of using an anonymous sperm donor, because she knew how carefully clinics screened donors for potential issues in their health history. The more she thought about it, the more confident she became that she could be a single mother.

There had been one small, unexpected snag in her plan. Shortly after the insemination process, an extremely apologetic director from the fertility clinic had called her to let her know that there had been a mistake. Instead of using a sample from a carefully vetted donor, the clinic had accidentally used sperm from a man who'd had cancer and had frozen his sperm due to the effects that chemotherapy could have on fertility.

At first, Willow had been alarmed at the news. She was shocked that the clinic could make such a mistake, and she was concerned that the donor hadn't been vetted for hereditary health issues. But the clinic informed her that the donor had been diagnosed with melanoma, a nonhereditary form of cancer. Willow's child would not be affected. Still, not only did Willow need to know what had happened, but they would have to inform the donor, as well.

Willow felt uneasy at the idea of the donor having any kind of involvement. But she knew that if their situations were reversed—if she had a child, somewhere out there, who was biologically hers—she'd want to know about it. There was nothing she could do to change the mistake the clinic had made, and the donor, whoever he was, probably felt just as shocked as she did. There was no use in casting blame, and ultimately, the only thing that mattered to her was that she had a healthy baby. She decided to give permission for the clinic to share her contact information with the donor, in case he wanted to discuss their extremely unusual circumstances, and in case he wanted the chance to get to know his child.

But the donor had never shown the slightest interest in meeting her. Not then, and not several months later, when she'd given her permission for him to be informed of Maisie's birth. As far as Willow was concerned, the donor had no interest in being part of their lives. Which was fine with her. It was how she'd planned it all along.

Aside from that one small mix-up, Willow's pregnancy had gone remarkably smoothly. She and Gran had both been completely besotted with Maisie from the moment she was born, and Gran had even put all of her savings into a trust fund for Maisie before she passed away. Willow had known that with Gran's good example to go on, she'd be able to provide her child with a loving home.

And as she watched Maisie traipse down the back steps with her bucket of sand toys, she couldn't imagine having done motherhood any other way. She wouldn't trade anything for the chance to meet the tiny person growing day by day before her very eyes. Maisie brought more joy to Willow's life than Willow could have ever imagined.

Willow thought that she and Maisie were getting on rather well in the world. Moving to the Caribbean had changed their lives for the better in every way. It might be far from all that was familiar in London, but London was fraught with memories of Jamie that Willow was happy to leave behind.

Willow's search for a change had led her to the Island Clinic on St. Victoria. At first, she'd been skeptical about the idea of working at a medical center that catered to celebrities. She'd become a nurse to practice medical care, not to tend to the whims of the A-list crowd. But she was drawn in by the clinic's commitment to helping its community, even providing care free of charge to island residents. And the motto fit with her own values—*We are always here to help.* Of course, it didn't hurt that the salary was more than twice what she was making in London.

As soon as she and Maisie had settled into their beach house, Willow knew she'd made the right decision. Their days were full of light and laughter, and Maisie was learning more about the world around her growing up on a Caribbean island than she possibly could have by spending her days in a North London day care.

She might not have the large family she'd always dreamed of, but she had Maisie, and that was enough. And on an island like St. Victoria, it was almost impossible not to know everyone. In many ways, her neighbors were like a family unit. Mrs. Jean, her nosy but well-meaning next-door neighbor, was always happy to watch Maisie along with her own grandchildren, and the island provided a sense of community Willow had never known anywhere else. At work, Willow's colleagues never failed to let her know that she was indispensable. She felt so close to her work friends that they seemed like a kind of family, too.

As for love… There were many different kinds of love, Willow thought. She certainly felt loved by the small circle of people in her life. But when it came to romantic love…well, she'd tried that, and it hadn't worked out very well. Willow still felt a pang in her chest whenever she remembered Jamie's words: *I thought you'd break up with me if you knew the truth.*

How could she ever tell if someone was just saying what they thought she wanted to hear, the way Jamie had? There was no way to know for sure. The only guaranteed way to protect herself was to decide that she was done with relationships, once and for all.

Willow had accepted that romance wasn't going to be part of her life. But not everyone on the island seemed as willing to accept that Willow had sworn off relationships.

Case in point: her neighbor, Mrs. Jean, was gathering rosemary from her small porch-side herb garden. Mrs. Jean seemed to feel it was her mission in life to see Willow settled in a relationship, and had a habit of willfully ignoring Willow's hints that this wasn't going to happen.

"Good morning," Mrs. Jean called as Willow approached. "I noticed that you and Maisie slept in a little."

Willow smiled. Maisie was a notoriously early riser. "Sleeping in" meant up by eight a.m. for the two of them. "Maisie was up a little later than usual last night, so we both needed some extra rest this morning."

Mrs. Jean's eyes twinkled. "Oh. I thought maybe you had a hot date and were sleeping in afterward."

"If your definition of 'hot date' is playing four games of Candyland in a row and then trying to wrestle an overtired three-year-old into the bathtub, then I'm guilty as charged."

Mrs. Jean snorted. "You spend all your time working and looking after Maisie. You need to take a little time for yourself once in a while."

"Ooh, is this an offer to babysit?"

"You know that Maisie's welcome over anytime. Why don't I watch her this Friday night and give you a break?"

"That would be great. I could really use a chance to catch up on some paperwork at the clinic."

Mrs. Jean gave her a pained expression. "I'm not offering to watch Maisie so you can do some paperwork. I want you to go out and have some *fun*. Go down to Williamtown and meet some young men. That's what I would be doing if I were your age."

Willow had her doubts about that. Mrs. Jean had eight children of her own, and numerous grandchildren. Even if she didn't know about the heartbreak Willow had faced, she should at least be able to understand that Willow didn't have time for dating between her full-time job and taking care of Maisie.

"Mrs. Jean, even if I had time in my life to date, you know as well as I do that there aren't too many single people to choose from on St. Victoria. I can't imagine how I'd meet someone new on an island this small."

At this, Mrs. Jean's eyes gleamed, and Willow realized too late that rather than ending the conversation, she'd given Mrs. Jean an opening.

"What about one of those nice doctors you work with?"

"Absolutely not. I could never date one of my colleagues. My job is important to me, and relationships make everything too complicated."

"Then what about one of those celebrities who are always coming to your clinic? Didn't that big Hollywood action star just have his gallbladder removed? You must have at least tried to get his number."

Willow couldn't help laughing. "If I don't want to complicate my job by dating a colleague, then I *definitely* don't want to complicate things by dating a patient. It'd certainly cost me my job."

"Who needs a job if you can snag yourself a movie star or an oil sheikh?"

"Mrs. Jean!"

The older woman rolled her eyes. "All right, I get it. You have principles, or some such nonsense. No dating patients. We'll just have to think of someone else for you."

"Sorry, Mrs. Jean, but even if I did plan to date again, I'm afraid it would be a hopeless case. Everyone on the island is either already taken or someone I work with. Or they're a neighbor or a friend."

"I wouldn't be so sure about that. What about that tall drink of water coming up the beach?"

Willow turned in surprise. Newcomers hardly ever came by the secluded stretch of beach she lived on. Yet less than twenty feet away, a tall man with light brown hair was picking his way over the sand. His crisp white shirt and tie were decidedly out of place in the Caribbean sunshine, and she could tell from his pale skin that he was unaccustomed to the sun. He was barefoot, with the ends of his trousers rolled up around his shins, and he carried his shoes and suit coat in one hand, and a briefcase in the other.

As the man approached, Willow noticed that his features were not altogether unattractive. His brown hair grazed his forehead in a way that made Willow want to sweep it from his eyes, which were a pleasing hazel. His frame was thin, but his gait suggested that he was used to carrying himself with the stance of a more muscular man. Willow found herself wondering if he were recovering from a long illness. Or perhaps he was simply unused to walking on hot sand—his pale skin suggested he didn't spend much time on the beach.

When he looked up at Willow, he smiled in greeting, and it was his smile that sent a jolt through Willow that she wasn't expecting. There was something about his mouth that caught her attention, although she couldn't quite put her finger on what it was. Perhaps it was the shape of his jaw—or maybe the way his chin curved—that made him seem extremely…kissable.

"Not bad, not bad," muttered Mrs. Jean.

The sound of Mrs. Jean's voice brought Willow back to reality, and she chided herself for having absurd thoughts about a complete stranger. As the man bent to speak to Maisie, her maternal instinct kicked in.

"Maisie," she called. "You know better than to talk to strangers."

She tried to make her voice sound stern, but she was terrible at being stern with Maisie. And strangers were such a rarity on this part of the island that her voice came out with more curiosity than sternness.

Now that she was at close range, Willow could see that the man looked more out of place than ever. Despite his pallor, she couldn't help noticing again that his hazel eyes were a striking complement to his sandy brown hair.

She wondered if he was a lost tourist, looking for directions to Williamtown. But in his stiff white shirt, he looked more like a solicitor than a tourist.

"Sorry to intrude," he said as she approached. "I was just complimenting this little one on such a fine sandcastle."

Willow recognized the clipped cadence of a North London accent, and things began to fall into place. Her first guess—that the man might be a solicitor—might be correct, after all. The trust that Gran had left for Maisie wasn't large, but it had been enough to ensure that Maisie would have a little bit of money to rely on if anything should ever happen to Willow. Back in London, a solicitor from the firm would check on Maisie once a year to ensure her well-being. Gran had felt that this was only practical, given that Willow and Maisie were alone in the world. She'd wanted to be sure that Maisie would always be supported, no matter what. After moving to the Caribbean,

Willow had assumed the firm would simply do these check-ins through video conference calls, rather than sending someone all the way out to the islands. But then, Gran had been a formidable woman. She'd probably threatened to haunt the firm from beyond the grave if they didn't do their due diligence where Maisie was concerned—and no one who'd ever met Gran would deny that she was capable of it.

"You must be from Camden," Willow said, naming the North London borough where her grandmother's firm was based.

He seemed surprised, but replied, "I am indeed from Camden. Theo Moore. I'm looking for Willow Thompson."

"Well, here we are. I'm Willow, and this is my daughter, Maisie."

For just a moment, Willow could have sworn the man was at a loss for words. She wondered if he was somewhat new at his job. Or perhaps he was simply tired from a long journey. But then he swallowed hard and seemed to recover. "Maisie," he said quietly. "You chose a beautiful name for her."

Willow couldn't help smiling. She loved saying Maisie's name. "We both think it suits very well, don't we, Maisie?" she said as the little girl gave a firm nod.

Theo paused for a moment, as though trying to recover himself. Willow realized that he must be exhausted.

"Did you come straight from the airport?" she asked.

"I did indeed. I'm terribly sorry to intrude in this way. I should have found some way to notify you that I was coming, but I only knew that you lived somewhere on St. Victoria. It did take a bit of detective work to track you down."

"I'm surprised to hear that. I thought I'd up-dated my new address with the firm when we moved."

He gave her a quizzical look. "The…firm, I suppose…had your old London address. I learned from your former neighbors that you'd moved."

Out of the corner of her eye, Willow could see Mrs. Jean approaching. "Why don't you come inside for some lemonade?" she said quickly. "Camden's a long way away, and I'm sure you're tired from your journey."

Again, he looked surprised, but said, "I'd love that. There's much for us to discuss, and it's probably best that we go over it all inside."

Willow couldn't imagine what there would be to discuss, as Maisie's yearly check-in vis-its were usually quite brief. She supposed that since this Theo Moore had traveled all the way from London, the visit would be longer than usual in order to justify the expense.

To her surprise, Maisie slipped her hand into Theo's as they walked toward the house. Theo didn't seem to mind. In fact, he appeared to be quite charmed.

Willow felt her heart do a flip-flop in her chest. *Settle down*, she told herself. She'd known the man for all of forty seconds, and yet here she was, ogling him like a teenager at a school dance. She forced herself to tear her eyes away from him and turn toward the house, hoping that he hadn't noticed her staring at him.

As they passed Mrs. Jean, she gave Willow a pointed look that Willow interpreted as *Don't screw this up.* Willow shot back a look that she hoped Mrs. Jean interpreted as *Quit making such a big deal out of everything.* The older woman snorted and sashayed back to her house.

Willow, Theo and Maisie stepped through the back door of Willow's beach house and into the kitchen, and Willow pulled a pitcher of lemonade from the refrigerator.

"I can help pour," Maisie said.

"The pitcher's too heavy, love. But you can take three big glasses from the cupboard." She glanced at Theo. "Maisie's at the age where she loves to help."

"I can see that," he replied as Maisie strained to reach the plastic glasses from a high cupboard. "I like to help, too. May I lift you up, Maisie?" He glanced toward Willow, who nodded her permission.

Maisie nodded, too, and Theo lifted her just high enough so that the little girl could take three glasses from the cupboard and set them on the kitchen counter.

"She must like you," said Willow. "Normally she's very big on doing things all by herself."

"I'm told I make a great first impression," he said, and Willow felt her knees weaken a bit as he smiled again.

She pulled a chair from the kitchen table to steady herself. "Why don't we sit down? I'm sure you'd welcome the rest after coming such a long way."

"Thank you." He sat beside her at the table and sipped his lemonade. "This is very kind of you. I haven't had anything to drink since the flight."

"It's no trouble at all. We Londoners have to look out for one another."

He waved at the beach outside the kitchen window. "This is a far cry from London."

"Yes, that was the idea."

"It's an interesting choice, to raise a child so far away from home."

She stiffened. It seemed an awfully forward thing for a solicitor to say. Strikingly attractive or not, this man had no right to judge her decision of where to raise Maisie, even if he was involved in managing Gran's trust. Willow was the sole person responsible for Maisie's care, and although she often wished she had more help, one of the benefits of being a single mum was that Willow didn't have to put up with anyone's judgment of her parenting. "St. Victoria is our home now," she replied. "It may be unconventional, but I believe the experiences Maisie has here are far more educational than anything she could get out of an overpriced day care in the city."

"I'm sure you're right," he said. "I simply meant that you do seem to be so far from family, here in the Caribbean."

"Family?" she said, looking at him quizzically. "What are you talking about? I thought the firm that managed Gran's trust knew perfectly well that Maisie and I haven't any other family."

Now it was his turn to look confused. "Trust?" he said. "What trust?"

"Gran's trust... Vera Brown's trust, that she had set up for Maisie before she died. Isn't that

what you're here to discuss? Aren't you a solicitor from the firm? A moment ago, when I
mentioned the firm, you said they had my old
London address."

"I'm afraid I wasn't entirely sure what you
meant by 'the firm.' I thought you might be
referring to the fertility clinic. The one you
went to...to have Maisie."

Willow's stomach went cold.

"I've been searching for you for months,"
he said. "The clinic gave me your last known
address, but it's been a few years, and it seems
you moved a few times. I eventually learned
that you lived on St. Victoria, and once I arrived, some helpful locals pointed me to the
right beach. They said if I just started walking, I'd run into you eventually."

She already knew the answer, but she forced
the question out, anyway, in a dry whisper.
"Why have you been searching for me for
months?"

"Because I needed to meet my daughter."

She shook her head. "You can't be saying
what I think you're saying."

"Yes. I'm Maisie's father."

CHAPTER TWO

WILLOW SAT AT her kitchen table, head spinning, as she tried to absorb Theo's words. She couldn't fit them in her mind in a way that made sense. Maisie didn't have a father. Maisie had Willow, the way Willow had had Gran when she was growing up. Their family was small, but special. And it did not include a father.

Even though she was sitting, she clutched the edges of the kitchen table to steady herself.

"I'm sure this is a lot to take in," said Theo. "I did ask the clinic to let you know that I was trying to get in touch, but all of the contact information they had for you was out of date. I suppose that's not surprising. It has been several years, after all."

Maternal instinct overrode Willow's shock, and she stood up and pulled back Maisie's chair. "Run along and play in your room, love. Mr. Moore and I need to talk."

"Can I bring my lemonade?"

"Yes, but hold the glass with both hands so you don't spill." Maisie took her glass from the table with two sturdy hands, her brow furrowed in concentration as she carried it to her room.

Theo gave Willow a pained expression. "You don't want her to see me."

Willow was surprised to feel a twinge of sympathy for this stranger in her kitchen. But she barely knew this man. Even if he were Maisie's father, she had no intention of letting him near Maisie until she knew a lot more about him. "It's nothing personal, Mr. Moore. It's just that I don't know anything about you, or why you're here."

"Please, call me Theo. I know that me showing up here must come as a shock. But I can explain everything—why I've showed up here so suddenly, and why I've stayed away for so long. Just hear me out, and afterward, if you want me to leave, I'll go. I'm just asking for a chance."

He'd kept his voice fairly steady, but as a nurse, Willow was used to listening to people in pain. She hadn't missed the note of anguish in his voice, and it touched her heart. She didn't know what had brought this man here, but she could see that, to him, it was a matter of desperate importance.

But she couldn't imagine what would be so important that he had to be here now, in person, when he'd never bothered to contact her before. Unless… Her heart rose in her throat. The clinic had told her that they'd used sperm from a donor who'd had a history of cancer, but they'd assured her it was nonhereditary. But what if there was some other, newly discovered health problem that Theo had come to warn her about? Something that could affect Maisie? She told herself not to panic. Whatever Theo was so desperate to speak about with her might be important, but there was no reason to assume the worst. Not yet, anyway.

He took a manila envelope from underneath the suit coat he'd been holding. As he moved, she thought she noticed again a slight awkwardness, as though he was used to moving with more bulk. Another worry crossed her mind: Was he here because something had changed with his own health? Had the cancer, perhaps, returned? His skin was so pale. On the beach, she'd thought he had the look of someone recovering from a long illness, and now, as she examined him with a professional eye, she wondered if that illness had been quite recent. Or perhaps was still ongoing. Despite having just met Theo, she felt a pang of concern for him. She might not know him at all, but his hazel eyes seemed so kind. Now that he was sitting across from her, he was close enough that she could make out flecks of gold in them.

Shocked as she was to see him here, she had only to look at him to see that he'd been through some suffering. And yet, she couldn't help noticing that for all his awkwardness his hands were steady and graceful as he opened the manila envelope and removed several documents. His eyes met hers, and their expression was hopeful, but determined. And he'd come such a long way. It couldn't hurt, she thought, to at least find out why he was here.

"All right, Mr. Moore," she said, gently emphasizing her use of his last name. "Why don't you start by proving that you're who you say you are."

His relief was palpable. "Easy enough," he said, handing her the documents from the envelope.

She took the papers with trembling hands, and spread them before her on the table.

Among other things, there were letters from the fertility clinic where she'd undergone treatments explaining the whole mix-up: how they'd intended to use sperm from a vetted donor, but had accidentally used Theo's frozen sperm instead. She remembered those letters all too well. She'd received very similar letters herself, with their apologies and explanations.

Willow remembered how shocked she'd been upon first learning that the clinic could make such a mistake. If she'd have wanted to she could have pursued legal action, but in the end, she'd decided that having a healthy baby was all that mattered, all she wanted. She didn't need to complicate that. And Theo's choice not to get in touch made that even easier. Once she'd learned that the insemination had been successful, she'd even given the clinic permission to contact Theo. And again, when Maisie was born, she'd given her permission for Theo to meet her. But he'd never responded.

Although she could see that the clinic had followed through: the envelope held a copy of the letter to Theo, informing him that he was the father of a healthy baby girl. There was even a copy of an ultrasound picture that she recognized. She had the original picture, framed, in her bedroom.

Even if Theo hadn't brought along all of this documentation, Willow would have known that he was telling the truth about being Maisie's father. All she had to do was look at Maisie. The little girl shared so many features with

Theo that seeing him was like seeing the missing pieces of a puzzle. Willow kept her eyes fixed on the documents: there was a copy of a photo ID of Theo, a work badge that identified him as a research oncologist at Regent's Hospital in London. He had longer hair in the picture, which made the features that he and Maisie shared even more evident. Willow had always thought that Maisie got her wavy hair from her, but the color, a light, sandy brown, was clearly Theo's. And Maisie's height—now there was another mystery solved. At three years old, Maisie was already half a head taller than every child in her preschool class, and as she took in Theo's frame, Willow could see why.

Theo was, indeed, Maisie's father.

Or at least, he was her biological father. He was a sperm donor, she reminded herself. Not a father.

She looked again at Theo's work badge from Regent's Hospital. "You're an oncologist?"

"Yes. I mainly do research, though I like to work with patients when I can. But there've been certain…unexpected changes that made clinical work difficult. In a way, I suppose that's how this all starts."

"Go on," she said.

"About four years ago, I was diagnosed with

melanoma. That's why I froze my sperm in the first place. My doctors advised that I take that step because chemotherapy can sometimes have an effect on fertility. I've always known that I wanted to be a father, so freezing my sperm was a safeguard."

Pieces were beginning to fall into place. She'd known, from the staff at the fertility clinic, that Theo had cancer, but his choosing not to get in touch meant she had no idea how he might have been getting on. And looking at Theo now, it was clear that the cancer wasn't far behind him. She estimated he was about thirty pounds underweight for his height and frame, and his sandy brown hair was quite short, as though it were just starting to grow back. She couldn't help feeling sympathetic. Cancer could be devastating, and the treatment took almost as much of a toll on the body as the illness itself.

"When I got the call from the clinic, informing me of the mix-up, I didn't know how to feel," he continued. "At first, I was outraged. It was such a grave mistake on their part. But then, as I got used to the idea, I realized that it might be for the best."

For the best? For a moment, she wondered if the Caribbean heat was affecting him. But then she recalled all the times she'd had that very same thought over the past three years. The mix-up was for the best, because if things had happened any other way, she wouldn't have Maisie.

But Theo couldn't have that perspective. He'd barely met Maisie, by his own choice. "How could you think such a serious mistake was for the best?" she asked.

"I know it sounds strange. But I'd always wanted to have children, and at the time, there was no way for me to be certain of whether that would ever happen. It might not have been how I'd ever pictured becoming a father, but it meant the world to me to know that she existed."

This definitely didn't fit with the impression of Theo she'd formed over the past three years. She'd pictured a man who wanted to put the clinic's mistake as far behind him as possible, dealing with the situation by ignoring it, and eager to avoid any commitment she might ask of him. He certainly didn't need to worry about that: legally, he had no claim to Maisie; his name wasn't on her birth certificate. His lack of contact with her had informed that decision. Willow needed nothing from him. But he spoke as though Maisie meant everything to him, even though he'd chosen not to know her.

She wondered if she would have felt differently if she'd known he was fighting cancer all this time. But that, she thought, was the heart of the problem. Theo had never reached out to explain his situation at all, until now.

"I wish I had known all this sooner," she said. "The fertility clinic told me about your medical history, but that didn't explain why you didn't reach out. As I never heard from you, even after you'd had two opportunities to be involved, I assumed you either didn't want a child, or didn't want Maisie." She tried to keep the note of accusation out of her voice. She sympathized with Theo's situation, she really did, but part of her wondered…what kind of man ignored his own child for three years? Even under the most extenuating circumstances?

"I can see why you might think that," he said, his voice tinged with emotion. "I hadn't planned to be involved, even though I wanted to be there very much. Staying away from Maisie is one of the biggest regrets of my life."

"Then why didn't you ever try to meet her? You could have explained your situation at any time during the past three years."

He gave an emphatic shake of his head. "No, I couldn't. It was hard enough being sick. I couldn't stand the thought of an innocent child—*my* child—being exposed to that much stress. And if treatment didn't…go well, then I didn't want to put my child through the grief of losing a parent."

He seemed to be trying to speak with a casual air, but Willow noticed the catch in Theo's voice as he acknowledged the possibility that treatment might not have been successful. There was so much unpredictability over the course of cancer treatment, so many times where all anyone could do was wait to see what happened next. Theo had been afraid for his life, she realized, and he'd had to make a difficult choice.

"I can't imagine what it would be like, to deal with cancer and then to learn you'd unexpectedly had a child," she said. "You made the decision you thought was best. So why come here now, after all this time?"

"Because I'm finally in remission. I started looking for you and Maisie as soon as I learned the good news."

A wave of relief washed over her upon hearing the word *remission*, and she realized she'd been anxious to know if his treatment had been successful. The relief she felt was real, even though she'd only known him a few moments.

But her thoughts were in turmoil. Everything Theo said was in direct opposition to the assumptions she'd made about him over the

past three years. On the rare occasions she'd
thought of Theo, it had been with cynicism and
some resentment for his complete lack of interest in Maisie. It wasn't that she necessarily
wanted his involvement; it was simply that his
apparent dismissal of her daughter amounted
to a rejection of the person she held most dear
in the world. And now she was learning that
his circumstances hadn't been what she'd
thought they were. For if what Theo said was
true, then he hadn't been ignoring Maisie. He'd
been trying to protect her.

And now, three years later, he was in remission, and he was here, hoping for…what
exactly? Did he expect to have any sort of relationship with Maisie? His next words confirmed her fears.

"I want to get to know my daughter," he
said. "I know I have no legal recourse, but I
am her father, and I came here hoping to find
some way to be involved in her life."

She was overtaken by a wave of feelings, including protectiveness toward Maisie, and jealousy at the thought of anyone else involved in
their close bond. When she'd become pregnant,
she'd never imagined sharing Maisie with anyone else. The thought of having another parent
involved in her daughter's life was completely
at odds with everything she'd envisioned for

the future. She certainly hadn't imagined having to deal with a man she barely knew arriving, unannounced, and declaring himself the father of her child. Not someone who, while pale and underweight, also had a devastatingly handsome smile and a pair of clear, hazel eyes that reminded her of the green and gold pebbles in the tide pools on the beach outside her home.

But no matter how interesting Theo's eyes were, his presence on the island would only be distracting for her, and for Maisie. Theo was a complicating factor that they didn't need.

Her life was proceeding just as she'd planned, and she didn't need any surprises now. Theo was right: he had no legal standing as Maisie's father. His name wasn't on her birth certificate. If she told him to leave, he'd have to go.

But Theo seemed so hopeful, and he'd been through so much. A part of her wished she could tell him that after all he'd been through, *of course* he was welcome into her and Maisie's lives. But however much she might sympathize with his situation, it didn't change the consequences of his decision. She had to think of her daughter first. Theo Moore was, by his own choice, a complete stranger to Maisie, despite their biological connection.

Still, he'd been in such an awful position, suffering all the uncertainty that came with facing a deadly illness. She didn't want to crush him completely, especially when he'd been in such a hard situation. She decided to let him down as gently as possible.

"I can understand why you feel it's important to get to know Maisie," she said. "It sounds as though it was very hard for you to stay away from her, although you did ultimately make the choice not to be involved."

"Because I wanted to spare her from any grief."

"I understand you were trying to do what you thought was right. But…it doesn't change the fact that Maisie is three years old now, and has no idea who you are. How would you even explain your relationship to her?"

His jaw tightened. "I'm her father."

"You might see it that way, but how can she? She doesn't know you at all."

"Which is exactly why I'm here. To form a relationship with her. To *be* the father I haven't been able to be all this time."

"But how would that even work? Practically speaking, I mean. Maisie and I have our lives here, on St. Victoria. Your life is waiting for you back in London. Four thousand miles away."

"I will find a way to make it work. I came here planning to do whatever it takes to be in my daughter's life."

"I can appreciate your determination, Mr. Moore. But you aren't thinking through the practicalities. How long were you even planning to stay in the Caribbean?"

"My return ticket is open-ended. I can stay for as long as necessary."

"But how long were you *planning* to stay?"

"I wasn't sure how you'd react to my arrival here. I thought perhaps…a week?"

"And then what? You'd fly back to London, while Maisie grows up here. You'd see her, perhaps, once or twice a year. I don't want to be harsh, Mr. Moore, but I have to protect my daughter, and I don't want her getting attached to someone who's just going to leave after a few days. And I really don't want her to get the impression that a father is someone who visits once a year."

"Then I suppose the way forward is clear. There's no other choice, really."

She breathed out in relief, glad that he could see how impractical it all was.

"I'll simply have to move to St. Victoria."

Her eyes widened. "You can't just decide to move to the Caribbean on a moment's notice."

"Why not? You decided to move here yourself."

"Yes, but I had researched positions abroad for nearly a year, and then chose the situation that I thought would be best for raising my daughter."

"And I'm trying to do the same. I've spent the past three years trying to do what's best for my child by staying away from her. And now that I'm finally in remission, I'm not going to waste my chance to be part of her life. This isn't an impulsive decision, it's an *easy* decision."

Theo was either reckless, crazy or…or, perhaps, he was as desperate to be involved in his daughter's life as he claimed to be.

He could also simply be telling her what he thought she wanted to hear, just as Jamie had. But Jamie's eyes had never blazed with determination the way Theo's did now, and his jaw had never been set with the same firmness.

She'd trusted Jamie, because she'd known him for years. But even though he'd said he wanted children, he'd never taken any action to back up his words. Theo, though, had tracked her down with limited information, and had flown four thousand miles with nothing more than hope for a chance to know his daughter. And even though it was hard to reconcile his presence now with his decision to stay away for so long, having cancer was one hell of an extenuating circumstance.

But could she trust him to be reliable? To be a suitable person for her daughter to have in her life? Without knowing him at all, how could she be certain of anything?

She thought it over for a long moment. Finally, she asked, "Why is Maisie so important to you?"

"What do you mean, '*why*'? She's my child."

"But do you know for certain that she's your only chance to have a child? Now that you're in remission, you could take a fertility test. Suppose you learned you could have other children? Would you really want to spend your life on a small island in the Caribbean, when there might be other options for you?"

He held her gaze for a long moment. "First of all, regardless of any children I *might* have in the future, Maisie is here now. Even if I were to have other children, she'd still be my daughter, and I'd still be determined to have a relationship with her, in whatever capacity you might allow.

"Second, the results of a fertility test won't be reliable until I've been in remission for at least a year. I don't know if Maisie is the only child I'll ever have, or if I'll get another chance.

But I don't need to wait another year to decide if I want to know my daughter. I've already had three years to think about her growing up without me, and I won't spend another minute without her if I can help it.

"And *third*, even though I haven't been with Maisie, she's been with me. Or at least, the idea of her has. Even though it was painful to think of her growing up without me, knowing that she was out there got me through some of the hardest days of my life. No matter what happens in the future, Maisie will always be important to me."

Willow almost believed that he meant every word. Almost. She had misgivings about whether he understood the commitment involved in being a parent, and whether he'd thought through what it would mean to make a permanent move to the Caribbean.

But he seemed determined to give it a try.

He'd had two chances to be involved in Maisie's life, and both times she'd thought his absence had spoken volumes. Could she give him a third chance? Especially now that she knew everything he'd gone through, just to be here, at her kitchen table?

His presence was a complication that she didn't want in her life. But something prevented her from telling Theo to leave. Maybe it was the sympathy she felt for all he'd been through. Maybe it was the determination in his voice and his expression. Or maybe, in spite of all the alarm bells going off in her mind, she wasn't done appreciating the exact shade of hazel in Theo's eyes.

Whatever the reason, she found herself saying, "If you're going to stay here, you'll need to find a job."

"I'm an oncologist."

"That's wonderful. I'm a nurse myself. But oncology is a profession, not a job. How are you going to earn a living here on St. Victoria? You'll need to have something that pays a salary and gives you a reason to stay here."

"Maisie is my reason for staying here."

"That's fine for right now, but what about next week? Next year? Island life isn't for everyone, and St. Victoria is small. How long before you get tired of the beach and start to miss your family and friends? How long before you start to resent Maisie for keeping you away from other work opportunities, other life opportunities, that you could have in London?"

"That would never happen."

Willow's mouth became a firm line. "The job is a deal-breaker. I need to know that you could see yourself living here long-term."

"You don't trust easily, do you?"

"Where my child is concerned, I don't trust anyone unless I have a good reason."

"Done. I'll get a job."

"And somewhere at least semipermanent to live."

"I'll start looking immediately."

Willow couldn't help but be impressed by his confidence. "I hope you understand where I'm coming from," she said. "I know you've been through a lot, and I'm so glad you're in remission. But you're a virtual stranger, and you're asking to be involved in my daughter's life. I can't risk her getting attached to someone who just wants to be around once in a while. Children need stability. Consistency."

His gaze pierced her from across the table. "And what about what *you* need?"

She felt disoriented, her heart and stomach doing jumping jacks together. Who cared about what she needed? As long as Maisie was taken care of, that was all that mattered. Except, when she looked into his hazel eyes, she felt a need that had nothing to do with groceries and roof repairs and everything to do with a growing warmth that she'd felt since the moment Theo entered the room.

"I have everything I need," she said curtly.

"What about financial support? You could at least let me help pay for Maisie's schooling, or for any necessities." He looked around the house, as though searching for any repairs he could offer to finance.

"We don't need money. My salary more than covers everything. All I need from you, Mr. Moore, is for you to show that you're someone who can be dependable. In case Maisie ever needs to depend on you."

"She can. I'll prove to her, and to you, that she can."

Willow hoped, from the bottom of her heart, that he was telling her the truth.

"You know what? I think that went about as well as could be expected. All things considered, I think you should feel good about this, Theo. I really do."

Theo pressed his hand to his temples, grateful that his twin sister, Becca, couldn't see the pained expression on his face over the phone. Ever the optimist, Becca had a tendency to stretch reality at times in her determination to put a positive spin on things. Her hopeful attitude had been helpful while he was battling some of his worst days with cancer. But her determination to look on the bright side of life meant that she sometimes didn't understand the magnitude of the obstacles he was facing.

He was back in his room at the Harbor

Hotel, a charming, hacienda-style inn filled with tourists. He'd called Becca as soon as he could to tell her about his conversation with Willow. Of all his siblings, only Becca knew that Theo had gone to St. Victoria in search of his daughter, or that he even had a daughter. When Theo had learned he was a father, even though he'd wanted to shout that news from the rooftops, he decided against telling his family because he knew they'd want to be involved. It had been hard enough for Theo not to make contact with his daughter, knowing that if he did, he could potentially put her through the grief of losing a parent at an early age. He knew that he wouldn't be able to withstand additional pressure from his family if they felt he should make contact. And so he'd only shared the news with Becca, the person he trusted most to respect his feelings.

But he wasn't quite sure he agreed with her assessment of what had passed between him and Willow. "You think it went *well*, even though the mother of my child isn't sure she wants to let me into my own daughter's life?"

"I think it's a good sign that she wants you to show you can be consistent and stable first. She wants to know that you're serious about this. Now it's only a matter of time before she sees that you want the best for your child, same as she does. You can't blame her for being careful. I'd feel the same if it were my own child."

He knew Becca was right. But part of him had hoped that, somehow, Willow would trust him right away. He ached to get to know his daughter better. When Willow had invited him inside for lemonade, his heart had skipped a beat as Maisie had casually slipped her hand into his. His daughter's hand. There was nothing on earth that would stop him from holding her hand again.

"It's just that when I saw my daughter today…" He paused, trying to gain control over his emotions. "It made everything so real. Everything the cancer took from me."

"But now you get to take it all back, one step at a time. Starting with the most important part of all—Maisie. Cute name, by the way."

"I like it, too."

"So what's the mum like?"

"She's a nurse. She seems nice, but I think I overwhelmed her by showing up so suddenly. We exchanged our contact information, so I'll call her as soon as I have a firm job offer and a place to live."

"That could take a while. Don't you want to call her a little sooner, just to keep her updated?"

"No. I think I should give her some space,

so we can get to know each other gradually. I don't want to screw this up."

"What does she look like?"

"She's beautiful," said Theo before he could stop himself. He instantly wished he hadn't said it. It was a sure way to get Becca to start making assumptions about Willow that had no basis in reality.

"Whoa."

"No, don't get any ideas. I wasn't trying to imply anything, I was just stating a fact. I just meant that she *happens* to be objectively beautiful." And friendly, and warm. Something about her demeanor had instantly put Theo at ease, nervous as he'd been about making his first impression. And she *was* beautiful. The waves of her rich, dark brown hair had framed her face in a way that made him long to pull her silky tresses through his fingers.

But he was here to meet his daughter, and nothing more. The situation was already complicated enough. Whatever attraction he might feel for Willow would have to be ignored.

"Look, I know you're hesitant to get back into the dating pool, but you can't put it off forever," Becca said. "You've always wanted a family. And so unless you want to find someone else who agrees to make use of the rest of the sample you stored in that sperm bank four years ago, you'll have to go on a date eventually."

"I'll cross that bridge when I come to it. For now, I'm not interested in dating anyone, least of all the woman who determines whether or not I'm able to see my own child. Besides, I still look…well, you've seen me. You know how I look."

"Theo. You look fine."

But he couldn't believe it. Every time Theo glimpsed himself in the mirror, it was a shock to see how much his body had changed as a result of his illness and treatment. He'd lost over thirty pounds, and his frame, he thought, looked positively gaunt. His skin was pallid, and his sandy hair had only just started to grow back in the past few months. He couldn't imagine that he would be an appealing prospect for anyone, let alone someone like Willow.

"Your body will adjust back to its old self in no time, now that you're not going through treatment anymore. And any woman shallow enough to let your appearance keep her from seeing your personality probably isn't someone who's right for you."

He wanted to appreciate Becca's loyalty, but she couldn't know how it felt for him to see his own body change so much over the past few years. Thinking about dating and relationships was the last thing he needed right now.

"There's actually something I have to ask you," he said, hoping a swift change of subject would distract Becca from her interest in his love life. "I really hate to put you in this position, but I need to borrow some money."

"Don't give it a second thought," she said. "Just let me know how much you need, and I'll get it to you."

He hated having to rely on his sister for money. It wasn't that he thought Becca would say no. She was a successful financier, and had readily offered her support during his illness. But having to ask for her help was one more reminder of all that the cancer had taken from him. It had been nearly impossible to hold a steady job over the past few years. As an oncologist with a strong research background, he was always able to find a job when he was healthy enough to work. But keeping his bank account in order hadn't been easy. He had enough to support himself, but not enough to find a house in the Caribbean on short notice.

"I'll need at least enough to put down for a few months' rent," he said.

"Of course. And you should get a long-term lease. The mum needs to know you're committed."

"But what if—"

"Theo, no. No more what-ifs. You can't put everything on hold because of what might happen. None of us knows how long we have. Look at Dad. Look at *you*. We've all got to live while we can, which in your case means borrowing some money from your fantastically well-to-do twin sister so you can find a suitable place to live."

"I'll start paying you back as soon as I get a job," he said. He hoped St. Victoria needed oncologists. Not that it mattered. He'd take whatever job he could find if it meant he could be with his daughter.

"I know you will. But in the meantime, I'm actually glad you asked. I think it's good for you to ask for some support once in a while, instead of trying to face everything by yourself."

"Thanks, Becca. I'll repay you for…for everything. Someday. I swear."

"Hey. What are savings accounts for, if not to help your brother move to a Caribbean island? Don't worry about money right now. Just focus on getting your life back to where it's supposed to be. Get things settled with your daughter so I can come and meet her."

"Thanks," he said again, and hung up the phone.

Becca was the only person in his family he'd

spoken to in several days, with the result that when he finally checked his phone, there'd been seventeen voice mails waiting for his response. As he'd spent the past week traveling and tracking Willow down, he hadn't spared much time for returning calls. Now, he had messages from his parents, siblings, aunts, uncles and various cousins, all eager to know where he was, what his availability was like for upcoming holidays and whether he had a moment to chat. So far, the only message he'd returned was Becca's. He'd probably have to delete the rest and apologize for not responding later.

He scrolled through his call history and saw that not all the voice mails were from family. There were several from his medical care team, as well. He played the next message to hear the concerned voice of his primary doctor.

"We're all so glad to see you're in remission, but the fight isn't over yet. Get in touch with me as soon as you can so we can schedule your first year of follow-up appointments."

He knew he should return the call, but he wasn't ready to return to talking about cancer yet. Cancer had taken up so much of his time and attention over the past four years. He wanted a moment to himself, to absorb the reality: he'd met his daughter. He'd laid eyes on her, talked with her, seen that she was real. And perfect.

Oddly, though he tried to focus on Maisie, he found that his thoughts kept drifting to Willow. He hadn't wanted to tell Becca, because he knew she'd get carried away, but there had been something about Willow's warmth that had made Theo feel instantly connected to her, even as she had explained her reservations about allowing him in Maisie's life. She'd been frank and straightforward about what she needed with him, and why. There was something about her that made him feel she was innately trustworthy.

Openness was a trait Theo admired in people, because he was terrible at it himself. Growing up in such a large family had made it difficult to have any privacy, let alone any secrets. As soon as one person found something out, everyone else knew. Some of his family took this in their stride, but Theo had always been more guarded than his siblings. As a child, he'd always hated it when something important happened to him and one of his siblings spread the news first, or when family gossip distorted actual events. He was quieter than his siblings, keeping most of his feelings to himself, with the exception of Becca. He'd been lucky that he had a twin to confide in. He and Becca had always been fiercely protective of one another's privacy.

And there were times when he did want privacy, so very much. He'd been diagnosed with cancer shortly after his father had been diagnosed with Alzheimer's, which had devastated his mother and siblings. His father was doing well so far, but Theo knew, when he'd been diagnosed, that he couldn't put his family through the threat of another loss. Not when there was so much to do surrounding Dad's care, and when his mother needed so much support. He'd downplayed the extent of his cancer as much as he could. It was just a touch of melanoma. There was a high survival rate, and no need to worry.

Only Becca had seen past Theo's lighthearted demeanor and recognized it as a coping mechanism. She hadn't pressed him to talk about his illness any more than he was ready to, but she'd stayed over at his apartment on the long nights when the side effects of the treatment were bad, and she called and checked in on him often. She always claimed she was just calling to say hello, but he knew better.

Even though it was hard for him to let people in, he was grateful he'd had Becca. And if he'd chosen to, he'd have had the support of his other family members, as well. He simply hadn't wanted to cause his family any more distress. They had enough to deal with in managing his father's care.

He wondered what had it been like for Willow to be a single mother for these past three years. Had she had anyone to turn to when she needed support? Had she wanted anyone?

Her green eyes had seemed to light up when she'd first seen him, not knowing who he was, but simply wanting to welcome a stranger and show him kindness. He wondered what it would take to get her eyes to light up like that again.

First things first. A house, a job and then… some sort of plan for his new life in St. Victoria.

He hadn't expected that his stay here would be permanent, but he'd meant it when he'd told Willow earlier that it was an easy decision. His choice had been made the moment he felt the warmth of Maisie's hand in his. If his daughter lived here, then so did he. He was used to life changing suddenly and unexpectedly. At least this time, the changes were in a direction that offered something good.

He decided he could wait until later to return his doctor's call. He deleted the voice mail, stuck the phone in his back pocket and went to ask the hotel concierge about where he could find a good real estate agent.

CHAPTER THREE

WILLOW WAS A little disappointed, but not too surprised, when a week passed without any word from Theo. They'd exchanged contact information with the understanding that he'd call when he got himself settled. *If* he got himself settled. Despite the confidence he'd shown, she couldn't help wondering if he'd given it some thought and decided that he wasn't ready to move his entire life to the Caribbean. She knew that a week wasn't much time to find a job or a place to live, but she'd assumed that if he intended to stay, then he would keep her updated on his progress. Instead, the past week had brought much of what she was used to hearing from Theo Moore: silence.

She hadn't mentioned his arrival on the island to anyone. She'd told Maisie that Theo was a friend who had come to visit, and that she didn't know if they would see him again. As each day passed and she still didn't hear from Theo, she became increasingly confident that she'd been right not to explain things further. For all she knew, Theo might not even be on St. Victoria anymore. Perhaps he'd seen the sense in her words as she'd explained why he couldn't simply burst into their lives out of nowhere.

Still, a part of her had hoped that he would follow through with all the things he'd said he would. He'd seemed so sure of himself, so resolute. But then, she knew from experience that people weren't always what they seemed.

During their conversation, she'd formed the impression that Theo was someone who didn't give up easily. The determination in the set of his jaw, the fire in his hazel eyes…she'd almost fallen for that easy confidence of his. But she'd clearly been right to keep her guard up, because despite his fine words and smoldering expression, he'd made no attempt to keep in touch with her.

She did find it rather grating that, once again, she'd offered Theo the chance to be part of Maisie's life, and his response was complete silence, just as it had been when she was pregnant and when she'd given birth to Maisie. Despite his assertion that he'd frozen his sperm because he'd always wanted children, perhaps he'd decided that the responsibilities involved in fatherhood were more than he was willing to take on.

She told herself it was probably for the best. It wasn't good for Maisie to have an unreliable father figure popping in and out of her life. Willow herself had grown up without a father, and she'd turned out all right. Gran had never dated anyone, and had certainly never suggested that Willow needed any sort of guiding male influence. She smiled to think of Gran dating. It was impossible to imagine. Willow had barely been a year old when her parents passed away in a car accident, and Gran had thrown herself so wholeheartedly into childrearing that Willow had always felt she'd had all the love and support she needed. Still, there were times when she'd wondered what it would be like to have her parents present. When she'd broken up with Jamie, for example, she'd wished she'd had a father she could go to for advice. Gran had been wonderfully supportive, but she couldn't exactly offer a male perspective. And now, with Theo popping up so unexpectedly, she felt again how helpful it would be to have a father of her own to consult.

But Gran had taught her to make do with what she had. And right now, all she had was her instinct that it would be better for Maisie to have no father figure in her life, rather than one who was unreliable.

Willow also thought it might be for the best that *she* did not have much more exposure to Theo, either. Even though she hadn't seen him for several days, her mind had an inconvenient way of recalling how his hair, short but unruly, seemed to spill over his forehead in a way that made her want to push back the locks that just brushed his eyes. And the way his mouth curved up at the corners, as though that warm smile were about to break over his face at any moment.

She told herself that she had *not* been attracted to Theo. He simply had an interesting face, that was all. With a warm smile. As shocked and confused as Theo's visit had left her, she hadn't been able to stop herself from thinking about that smile over the past several days. Which left her all the more relieved that he hadn't contacted her again.

Between working full-time and raising a daughter on her own, Willow had always told herself that she was too busy to find a place for love or romance in her life. It was just as well that she hadn't felt an attraction to anyone in years, because work and Maisie kept her very busy. Not just busy, but safe. She'd never questioned her decision to be done with relationships after the breakup with Jamie. She'd trusted him for years, and in the end, not only had she been deeply hurt, but all of her dreams for the future had almost been lost. She couldn't risk that happening again, especially now that she had a child.

She felt another burst of irritation with Theo. What kind of a person confidently agreed to the conditions under which he could see his own child, and then disappeared without any communication for a week? Even if he'd decided to leave, he could have at least called to let her know he'd changed his mind.

She could understand if he was disappointed to learn that being involved in Maisie's life might be harder than he'd thought. But unless he had a place to live, a job and a plan for how he was going to be consistently present for Maisie, then Willow couldn't allow him to see her. Parenting was a huge commitment. Willow knew that none of the things she'd asked Theo to do were easy, because *she'd* done all of those things. She'd been doing them from the moment Maisie was born. And that really was the point. She knew what it took to be a parent, and she couldn't accept anything less for her daughter.

Of course, she could understand all he'd been through. Cancer wreaked such havoc and destruction on people's lives. She was so glad he was in remission. But that didn't mean he was ready to take on the reality of raising a child.

As she walked into work, Willow decided that she wasn't going to worry about Theo Moore any longer. She was tired of waiting for an update from him, and of worrying about the impact his presence would have on her life and Maisie's.

It's been over a week, she thought. *Surely if he were going to stay, I'd have heard from him by now. It's time to stop worrying about it, and to let things get back to normal.*

And she did, indeed, have a wonderful sense of normalcy as she headed into the nurses' station. She loved her job, and throwing herself into her work was one of her favorite ways to take a break from worrying about her own problems. She'd always found that when she was immersed in a medical procedure, her own worries drifted away as she focused on the task at hand. A few routine procedures were just what she needed.

When Willow had taken her job at the Island Clinic, she'd been looking for a way to make a drastic change in her life. She'd hoped that the job would allow her to have better work-life balance, and more time with Maisie, but she'd never dreamed that she would end up loving her job as much as she did. Willow had always been a caring and compassionate nurse, but in North London, she'd also been overworked, burned out and struggling to make ends meet. Most of her colleagues were in the same position. Now that she was working at a clinic where the salary more than met her needs, and where her colleagues were excited to come to work each morning, Willow discovered a new sense of enthusiasm for her profession.

At first she'd been nervous about whether she'd fit in at the Island Clinic. She was a practical person who had entered nursing because she wanted to care for those in need. But at the clinic, some of the clientele had faces that were almost as familiar to Willow as her own. Patients routinely arrived with an entourage and lists of extremely specific demands, including everything from dietary preferences to the kind of music played in exam rooms.

But even though the clinic catered to the well-known and the wealthy, it also strove to meet the needs of the island's residents, as well. The staff took the clinic's mission statement seriously: *We are always here to help.* No patient was ever turned away from the clinic due to their inability to pay. The clinic often shared patients with nearby St. Victoria

Hospital, taking on difficult cases or patients whose care might be too costly for the hospital. Willow was more than willing to put up with the quirks and demands of entitled celebrities from time to time, if it meant that the people of St. Victoria—people who were now her friends and neighbors—had the medical care they needed.

As she began to review the day's medical charts, she had to admit that after more than a year of working at the clinic, she was coming to appreciate many of its perks. The same luxury experiences the clinic strove to provide to patients tended to spill over onto the staff. Willow could and had worked under all kinds of conditions, and she didn't need luxury to be an effective nurse. But she certainly didn't mind that the coffee she sipped during her chart review came from a French press, or that the lunches she ate with her colleagues each day were prepared by a chef who'd earned three Michelin stars. In fact, she was almost starting to get used to it.

She looked up from her chart to take in the view from the big picture window outside the nurses' station. She'd never get used to the constant presence of white sand and palm trees, and she was glad of that. The view of the ocean was every bit as breathtaking as it had been the day she arrived.

She heard a buzz of voices as three nurses headed toward the station, deep in excited conversation. "Willow!" gasped Talia, a fellow nurse. "Have you heard? There's a rumor that Roni Santiago is on her way to the clinic!"

Willow couldn't help raising her eyebrows. Even though she was used to celebrity patients by now, Veronica Santiago—or Roni, as she was known by nearly everyone on earth—would be one of the most famous patients ever to arrive. Roni had begun her media career decades ago as a daytime talk show host. Her program was known to delve deeply into serious social issues, going far beyond typical sensationalism and fluff. She developed a reputation for bringing out deep emotions among her program guests and audience members. She'd also been known, and perhaps especially loved, for her frequent giveaways. Once, she'd gifted her entire studio audience with a weeklong cruise on the Baltic Sea. Since then, she'd founded a global nonprofit organization as well as her own media empire. There was a Roni magazine, a streaming TV channel and a lifestyle website where members could engage directly with Roni and with each other.

"Isn't it exciting?" said Talia. "My mother

and I used to watch her show together after I got out of school. I've always wanted to meet her."

Under other circumstances, Willow might have shared in Talia's excitement. But she'd been hoping to get wrapped up in some straightforward medical procedures. A few days of setting broken bones and mending lacerations would help her to get her mind off the turmoil that Theo's arrival had caused. She'd been in charge of coordinating celebrity care before, and in her experience, it usually meant not much medicine and a lot of babysitting. A guest with as big a name as Roni's was bound to arrive with her own list of special demands in addition to the luxury the clinic already offered. Willow hoped that she would be able to stay out of Roni's way and focus on providing medical care, rather than meeting the needs of a celebrity who was likely used to getting her own way most of the time.

Those hopes were dashed moments later when her boss, Dr. Nate Edwards, arrived at the nurses' station.

Nate was chief of staff at the Island Clinic, and Willow had developed tremendous admiration for him over the past year. When she'd first arrived in the Caribbean, his warmth and patience had helped Willow overcome any lingering doubts about her decision to move to St. Victoria. When she'd first read about the Island Clinic, she'd been intrigued by the location and the high salary. But it had been Nate's personality that confirmed for her that she was going to take the job. Nate's demeanor, driven yet down to earth, had convinced her that the clinic was sincere in its mission to help. She'd worked with him long enough to know that she could always trust him to do what was best for the clinic, the staff and their patients.

Which was why she felt her heart sink when he said, "Willow, I was wondering if you'd be willing to take the lead on coordinating Roni Santiago's care when she gets here."

"Are you sure you don't need me somewhere else?" she asked, desperately trying to think of an excuse. "Wouldn't I be more use in surgery? Or in the infectious disease wing?"

"I know looking after celebrities isn't your favorite part of the job. But Roni is in a somewhat unusual situation. She began chemotherapy for breast cancer a month ago, and since then, someone either in her entourage or on her treatment team has been leaking information to the press. A lot of it has been sensationalized—the tabloids make it sound as though she's on death's door."

"That's terrible," said Willow. "I had no idea

Roni Santiago had cancer. And I'm sure the reports in the news aren't good for her physical or emotional health."

"I'm surprised you haven't heard—it's been all over the tabloids."

"I never pay much attention to those," she said. That, and she'd so been preoccupied with thoughts of Theo's visit that she hadn't had much time to think of anything else.

"The paparazzi have been a serious problem. They're hounding Roni at every turn. She and her doctors agreed it would be best for her to come here, for the sake of security and privacy. We'll all need to be extra careful. I want her to be able to focus on rest and recovery."

"Is there any danger of the press finding out she's coming here?"

"The director of her previous cancer treatment center has assured me that no one at their end could *possibly* have revealed that Roni is headed our way, so we should be able to maintain her privacy without worrying that we'll be inundated by paparazzi. Still, caution is important. The press has been relentless."

"I'm sure that doesn't help with her emotional state." It was crucial for cancer patients to keep their spirits up. Still, Willow had been hoping for a brief respite from celebrity nursing. "Are you certain you need me to be the one to coordinate her care?" she asked Nate.

"If you don't mind. For one thing, you live off-campus. In the unlikely event that the paparazzi become a problem, it'll be less pressure for Roni and the staff if those involved in her care are able to leave at the end of the day."

Willow nodded. Being able to leave her work at work was one of the primary reasons she'd opted not to live in the clinic's on-campus housing.

"To tell you the truth, I have some ulterior motives in wanting Roni's care to be coordinated by one of our best nurses."

Willow couldn't help smiling at the compliment. She cared about what Nate thought of her, and it meant something to be held high in his regard.

And she didn't have to think very hard about what his ulterior motives might be. Nate was passionate about the clinic's mission to serve the island, especially to provide care to those who couldn't afford to pay. Even though the high fees paid by celebrities helped to offset the clinic's outreach work, Nate was always on the lookout for opportunities to encourage donations from high-profile patients.

"You're hoping she'll make a donation, either to us or to St. Victoria Hospital," she said.

"I certainly am. In fact, if Roni can see all the potential she has to help people on the island, then I'm hoping she'll consider sending some people from her nonprofit foundation out here, to help support the community even further. And…there's something else, too."

Willow waited. Nate looked around to make sure that no one else was listening. Then he turned back to her and said, "The thing is… I'm a huge Roni fan."

"What?" Willow laughed, not at Nate, but because she was surprised. He hardly fit the profile of Roni's core fan base, which tended to be a bit older, and mostly female.

"It's true. I grew up watching her show. Our housekeeper had it on every day when I came home from school. My family wasn't especially into big emotional discussions, or really *any* emotional discussions. So when I saw Roni's show, I was instantly hooked. Her guests and the people in her studio audience didn't even know each other, and yet they talked more about their feelings in five minutes than my family did in the average month. And Roni always tackled the real issues. There was nothing she shied away from. I think Roni Santiago might be personally responsible for a good ninety percent of my emotional development as a teenager."

"Wow," said Willow. "I'd never have taken you for a Roni fan."

"One of her biggest." Nate tapped his messenger bag. "This bag was on Roni's list of Favorite Fall Must-Haves two years ago. I've been using it ever since. Her recommendations never let me down."

Willow couldn't help smiling. "All right. If this one is important to you personally, then it's personal to me, too. I'll do everything I can to make sure she has a good experience here."

Nate beamed in gratitude. "I know you will."

"Meanwhile, I haven't seen a chart for her yet. Is her previous treatment center faxing her medical records?"

Nate pulled a chart from his bag and handed it to Willow. She thumbed through it, mentally gathering the essentials. "This is her second bout with breast cancer?"

"Yes. She had a bout of it eight years ago and went into full remission."

"It looks like she got lucky the first time. Just surgery to remove the tumor, and a few rounds of radiation. No chemo."

"The tumor was less than one centimeter, fully encapsulated when they caught it. Things are still looking good for her this time. They caught it fast, and she's already started chemo. In addition to the extra privacy, she and her doctors thought that a relaxing setting like ours would be helpful for her. Chemo takes a toll on the body, after all."

Willow nodded. Chemo was a terrible treatment, but if one absolutely had to undergo chemotherapy...well, she couldn't think of a better place than an island paradise with world-class doctors on call.

"Actually, there's one other piece to this that I wanted to talk over with you. We've just hired a new oncologist, and naturally he'll be the attending physician on Roni's case."

Willow felt a sudden sense of dread. *No*, she thought. *It's not possible.*

She held the edge of the counter at the nurses' station for balance as her knees had suddenly become unreliable and threatened to give out from under her. She swallowed hard, forcing herself to get the words out. "A new oncologist? What about Dr. Armstrong?"

"She's been talking about retirement for a while. She wants to cut back on her hours so she can spend more time with her family. This new guy is the perfect solution—he wants to focus on research, so both he and Dr. Armstrong can work part-time. It's win-win for everyone—we get a top-notch cancer researcher, Dr. Armstrong gets to cut back on her hours and we're still able to meet our own patients' needs while taking on those from St. Victoria Hospital. Also, he's pretty nice. I think you're going to like Theo Moore."

As if on cue, Willow saw the double doors behind Nate swing open, and Theo walked in.

He strode toward the nurses' station, nodding at Nate. His eyes widened as he saw Willow. Willow steeled herself, trying to maintain her outward veneer of calm, even though she felt as though the room was spinning. Somehow, when she had told Theo he needed to get a job, it had never crossed her mind that he might work *here*. She hadn't even known the clinic was looking to hire a new oncologist.

And if she had, would she have told Theo? A firm *no* welled within her in response. She couldn't possibly work with him. There was the complicating factor of his relationship to her as Maisie's biological father, which put him in the unusual position of being a complete stranger, yet also connected him to her.

And then there was the matter of his eyes. They were quite problematic, standing out as they did from the few locks of hair that fell from his forehead and just brushed against them. Why didn't he simply push the hair out of his eyes? Her fingers gave an involuntary twitch as she fought a momentary impulse to do it for him.

She reminded herself that she was a very busy single, working mother who didn't have time for distractions. She could understand how some women might find Theo attractive, but she was too busy to care about the way Theo's tousled hair fell over his forehead.

She definitely didn't have any attention to spare for his mouth and the way it creased up at the corners.

Then he smiled, and she caught her breath.

Dammit, she thought. No matter how busy she was, there was no way around it: Theo was an undeniably attractive man. And now, apparently, he was her undeniably attractive coworker.

Theo hadn't meant to get a job at the same clinic as Willow. The moment he stepped into the clinic and saw her, he was gripped with the fear that he might have made a terrible mistake. She'd told him she was a nurse, so it was a fair guess that she worked at one of the major medical centers on the island. But the past few days had been a whirlwind of job searching and house-hunting for Theo, and he'd never stopped to consider the possibility that he and Willow could end up working together.

He'd inquired about a job at St. Victoria Hospital first. Their head oncologist, Dr. Burke, had explained that they didn't have the budget for an additional oncologist, but had introduced him to Nate Edwards. Nate had been thrilled to meet Theo, and he was even more thrilled when he learned about the cancer research that Theo had been involved in. As the head oncologist at the Island Clinic wanted to reduce her hours before retirement, Nate offered Theo a position that would involve research and part-time clinical work at the clinic.

At first, Theo had been hesitant about working at a clinic that catered to celebrities. But as Nate explained it, he'd also be expected to take on patients from St. Victoria Hospital when needed. And the research component of his job would allow him to create grant proposals and research trials that would expand the treatment offered by the hospital. Theo liked the idea of having ample time to do research and pro-bono work, and he also liked the clinic's mission to ensure that no one was turned away, regardless of their ability to pay.

But Willow's presence was a complicating factor that he hadn't accounted for. All of the excitement he'd felt at the thought of calling to tell her he'd found a job drained away the moment he saw her at the nurses' station.

"Theo!" Nate clapped him on the shoulder.

"We were just talking about you. Come meet one of our best nurses."

"We've met," said Willow, her clipped tones confirming Theo's worst fears.

"Really? How—" But at that moment, Nate was paged overhead to the trauma wing. "Duty calls. I'll have to let you two catch up with each other on your own. We can touch base on the Santiago case later. And I want to hear about how you already know each other!" Nate flashed a grin and sped off.

Theo took a deep breath and tried to smile at Willow. "That should be an interesting conversation. What should we tell him?"

"Maybe first you can tell *me* what you're doing here!"

Theo gestured toward his white coat. "You said I needed to find a job. Well, here I am."

She closed her eyes, and Theo said, "Look, I understand. I had no idea that you worked here, and if I'd known, I would have turned the job down and figured out something else. But I think there's a strong upside to this. You're cautious about introducing me to Maisie because I'm essentially a stranger to both of you, right? But if we're working together, I won't be a stranger for very long. We'll get to know one another in no time."

"Yes, but…that's just it. You coming here…

wanting to be in Maisie's life…and now *working* at the same clinic—it's just a lot to take in all at once. And you haven't even tried to get in touch with me since last week."

Damn. Becca had been right; he should have called Willow sooner.

"I'm sorry," he said. "I didn't want to bother you with too many updates before I had everything settled. And I wasn't sure how often you'd want to hear from me. I didn't want it to seem as though I was trying to force myself into your life. Although…" He waved his arm at the clinic. "I guess my plan to give you space didn't work out the way I hoped it would."

She sighed. "It's not your fault. I should have seen this coming. If I'd given it any thought, I would have realized that you were bound to end up here or at St. Victoria Hospital. I was just so shocked when you arrived that I didn't even think of the chance that you could end up working here. But I would have appreciated some updates over the past week. When I didn't hear from you, I thought you'd decided to leave."

He could feel his stomach roil in protest. Leave? When he'd barely begun to get to know his daughter? Willow didn't know him at all.

But then, that was the problem. The fact

that Willow didn't know anything about him was the biggest obstacle he faced in getting to know his daughter.

"I'm not going anywhere," he said. "And I promise that working here won't interfere with our personal lives. I'm just here to do my job, and I'm sure you are, too."

She was about to respond, but at that moment, there was a burst of activity through the hospital's main doors. A throng of reporters surrounded a woman in a wheelchair as she was being pushed into the clinic. Each reporter shouted their questions so loudly that it was impossible to hear any of them clearly. Cameras snapped and chaos erupted as the press was shooed away by medical staff, only to swarm back toward the woman in the wheelchair while members of her entourage tried to protect her. Amid it all, a small French bulldog ran in circles, barking wildly.

Roni Santiago had arrived.

CHAPTER FOUR

WITHIN SECONDS, THE lobby of the clinic was packed with reporters, medical staff and members of Roni's entourage. A TV news crew was attempting to set up a camera in one corner, ignoring the arguments of a nurse, and the woman pushing Roni's wheelchair had to shove at reporters to keep them away.

"Call security," said Willow. Another nurse, who'd wisely decided to cower behind the nurses' station, nodded and began dialing. Willow headed toward Roni, but not before a reporter stuck a microphone in front of her face. "Miss, what's it like to have Roni herself at the Island Clinic? Are the rumors that she has a deadly, inoperable cancer true?"

So much for maintaining Roni's privacy. There was either a leak in Roni's entourage, or someone from her previous treatment center had revealed her transfer to the Island Clinic. Either way, the press had followed her here, and now it would fall on the clinic staff to control the damage.

"Our patients' medical histories are confidential, and you need to leave, now," said Willow, barely concealing the irritation in her voice.

To her absolute shock, as she tried to move toward Roni, the reporter grabbed her arm in a tight grip and shouted, "Just a few more questions, please!" She tried to shake him off, but his grip was like a vise, and she nearly lost her balance trying to twist away from his grasp.

Theo moved so quickly that she barely saw him. One moment the reporter had hold of her arm; the next, his microphone had clattered to the floor, and Theo was holding the reporter's shoulder in a firm grip. Theo twisted the reporter's arm behind his back and steered him away from Willow. The expression on Theo's face was so furious that Willow wasn't sure what might have happened next had a uniformed security guard not arrived to take hold of the reporter.

More security officers arrived to herd the press back outside the clinic. Willow could see that Roni was barely conscious.

"We need to take her back to an exam room immediately," she muttered to Theo.

"I'll show you the way, if you can get us through this crowd."

Theo put one arm around Willow's shoulders to protect her as he cleared a path through the crowd. She appreciated his tall frame, which provided shelter from the mob. As the security officers pressed the reporters back, Theo and Willow made their way to the woman who was pushing Roni's wheelchair.

"Are you family?" Theo asked her.

"I'm her best friend. Siobhan."

"All right, you take the dog, I'll take over wheelchair duty." Theo and Willow guided Roni's chair into an exam room as her friend picked up the French bulldog, which immediately stopped barking. Roni seemed as though she could barely lift her head, and as Willow began her examination, she could see that Roni was drifting in and out of consciousness.

"How long has she been like this?" Theo asked Siobhan. Willow noticed that his voice was firm but calm, with no trace of the fury she'd seen in his expression a moment ago.

"About fifteen minutes. We were talking on the plane, and then all of a sudden she just started…drifting off. I thought she was losing consciousness, but she comes around every couple of minutes or so. I can't believe the press followed us here. The whole point of coming was to have some privacy."

"Security will get things under control," Willow reassured her. "Roni will have the rest and privacy she needs."

From her wheelchair, Roni gave a low chuckle. "Thank God for that."

"Roni?" said Willow. "Can you hear us?" But Roni had once again dropped her head to her shoulder and closed her eyes.

Willow nodded at Theo. "Mild seizures, possibly in response to high fever."

"Give me the history," he said.

"Latina woman in her early sixties, current diagnosis of breast cancer, recently started chemotherapy. No known allergies. Presents with seizures and possible high fever." Willow checked her thermometer. "Temperature of one hundred and five. Seizures are persistent but seem to have slowed. Shall we order testing? It could be a seasonal flu, or a bacterial infection she picked up while traveling."

He paused. "She's already started chemo?"

Willow glanced at the chart. "According to her records, she started a few weeks ago. It looks as though she was about halfway through the first planned round of chemo before she decided to transfer her care here."

"Then let's order the testing, but start her on a fever reducer and antibiotics right away."

Theo leaned in toward Roni's wheelchair. "Roni?" he said gently. "Can you hear me?"

Roni's eyes fluttered open.

"Roni, you most likely have a case of febrile neutropenia. That means your body is having a strong reaction to chemotherapy, and it hasn't been making enough of the white blood cells you need to fight off a bacterial infection. The good news is that your friend got you here fast enough for us to start antibiotics within two hours of your fever, which means that you should begin feeling better right away."

"Sounds like I got here just in time," Roni croaked.

"Not a moment too soon," Theo agreed, and Willow noticed again the way the corners of his mouth seemed to tug upward as he spoke. "We still need to wait for the test results to be sure, but we're going to start the antibiotics right way. Odds are good you'll be feeling better very soon."

Of course, Willow thought. Febrile neutropenia. No wonder Theo hadn't wanted to wait for test results. Starting a patient on antibiotics within two hours of the outbreak of a fever could have a significant impact on treatment outcome. Thanks to Theo's quick thinking, Roni was probably going to be fine.

She considered what he'd said only a few moments ago—that working together might allow them to get to know one another more quickly. She still wasn't certain of how she felt about that. But she was glad of the chance to see that Theo was a competent doctor. And although she was certain she could have handled the situation herself, she did appreciate the way he'd pulled that reporter off of her without a moment's hesitation.

So far, Theo had proved that he knew his field well, and that he had her back. She grudgingly admitted to herself that both of those were qualities she valued greatly among her coworkers.

She just wished her stomach wouldn't do flip-flops as she watched him write orders in Roni's chart.

"There's a suite waiting for both of you, but we need to keep her in the exam room for a few hours of observation," she said to Siobhan, trying to pull her focus back to her patient. "You're welcome to stay with her until then."

"Can she keep the dog with her?" asked Siobhan.

Willow hesitated. Dogs typically weren't allowed in exam rooms, but Roni's French Bulldog had settled down considerably, curling quietly into her lap. She smiled and touched a finger to her lips. "I suppose it's fine. But keep it quiet."

As they left the exam room together, Theo said, "Wow. Is it typically like this, with the press?"

"Actually, it's extremely rare. We all take discretion very seriously here. My guess is that someone on Roni's team leaked the information that she was coming. It may not even have been an intentional leak. Some of our patients get so much scrutiny from the press that a careless word, dropped at the wrong time, can tip off the news media to things they aren't supposed to know. Fortunately, we do have excellent security personnel. They're very good at keeping the sharks away. As are you apparently. I want to thank you for helping me out with the reporter back there."

His eyes grew stormy again, and for a moment she thought she saw a trace of the anger that had clouded his face earlier. But it quickly passed as he said, "The important thing is that you're all right." He searched her face carefully. "You *are* all right, aren't you?"

"I'm perfectly fine." Despite herself, she rubbed her arm. It did still hurt a bit. The reporter's grip had been firmer than she'd realized. She hoped she wasn't going to have a bruise.

Theo frowned. "If they're going to be that bold, we should talk to Nate about increasing security for the staff as well as for Roni."

"Certainly, if it makes you feel better. But I know Nate. He won't tolerate an intrusion into a patient's privacy without swift action." And then, in spite of herself, she laughed as she remembered her own first week at the Island Clinic, just over a year ago. "If you think that was bad, you should have been here last year. We had an entire K-pop group."

"K-pop?"

"Korean pop music. Picture five teenage boys, all on the verge of international stardom. Some of the dance moves they do are pretty complex, and apparently they'd been attempting an illegal pyramid formation on a high stage that collapsed, resulting in multiple compound fractures. Their manager didn't want word getting out that they'd been practicing moves banned in Korea, so he had them flown here for absolute privacy."

"But word got out they were here?"

"Through no fault of ours. One of the boys posted a picture of the view from his room online, and a fan from the island realized he was probably somewhere on St. Victoria. It's a small island, and with every woman under twenty on the lookout—well, it was only a matter of time before they determined by process of elimination that the band members were here."

"It was bad, huh?"

"Never underestimate the detective work of teenage girls. Every young woman on the island started trying to get a glimpse of them at the clinic. One of them actually succeeded by disguising herself as a delivery driver. But don't worry. After a while you'll see that these kinds of incidents are really extremely rare."

"I see. So...does this mean you've come around to the idea of us working together?"

She told her stomach to stop doing flip-flops. "I suppose it won't hurt to give it a try. You made a good call with Roni back there. And I liked how you discussed her treatment with her."

"How's that?"

"You told her that the odds were good that she would feel better soon, but you didn't make any false promises. You were confident, without overselling or twisting the truth."

He nodded. "That's important with cancer patients. Everything's about what the odds are. You have to talk about chances, rather than promises. And you have to talk about statistics without making a person *feel* like one."

She was certain he was speaking from his experience as a patient. How important it must be to him, she realized, to be able to use his firsthand knowledge of how it felt to have cancer to help his patients.

Nate's words from earlier that morning came back to her: *I think you're going to like Theo Moore.* She wondered if that could possibly turn out to be true.

She broke from her reverie to notice that he was staring at her.

"What is it?" she asked. She looked at her nurse's coat, trying to see if she'd spilled coffee somewhere.

"It's just…" He took a deep breath, and his words came rapidly, as though he were forcing himself to push them out. "Speaking of statistics. I was wondering. What are the odds you might have dinner with me later this week?"

For one brief, wild moment, she almost thought that Theo was asking her out on a date. But then she realized that couldn't possibly be the case. Given the circumstances between the two of them, a date was out of the question.

Still, it couldn't hurt to clarify. "When you say, 'have dinner with me,' what exactly do you have in mind?"

He gave her a quizzical look. "Well, I suppose by 'have dinner,' I'm anticipating that there'd be food involved, most likely eaten in the evening, and the 'with me' part implies that it'd be the two of us, eating that food together."

She rolled her eyes. "Yes, but it's *just* dinner, right? It's not…a date?"

"Oh, no, not at all," he said without any hesitation. "I hope it didn't sound as though I was suggesting a date. Especially considering our situation. My priority is getting to know Maisie, after all."

She blushed. *Of course* he hadn't intended to suggest a date. He'd traveled four thousand miles and uprooted his life for the chance at being involved with his daughter; the last thing any reasonable man in his situation would do was put everything at risk with romantic entanglements. And she had no reason to believe he was attracted to her.

She was glad he couldn't read her thoughts, because in spite of the fact that she knew perfectly well that it would be a mistake to date Theo, her spirits had plummeted when he'd explained he was asking her to dinner with no romantic intentions whatsoever. While she wished he hadn't jumped to clarify his lack of interest in her quite *so* quickly, it was probably fortunate that his intentions were strictly platonic. She was too busy, and the risks were far too high. Life was complicated enough without adding heartbreak. Not to mention how confusing things could be for Maisie. Even if Theo had been interested in her, he'd have been off-limits to Willow for that reason alone.

But Theo was right about one thing. She needed to get to know him better. He was clearly making a concerted effort to build a life for himself on St. Victoria. If she intended to give him a fair chance, then she'd need to see him more often.

Maybe dinner wasn't such a bad idea.

"I suppose it couldn't hurt," she said.

"I should hope not. Who knows? It might even be fun."

Dammit. His hazel eyes positively twinkled when he smiled like that. Despite herself, she smiled back, even as her mind continued to resonate with phrases like *off-limits* and *totally inappropriate* and *probably not even interested, anyway.* She told herself to listen to the wisdom of those words.

"What time?" she heard herself say.

Four days later found Theo trying, desperately and unsuccessfully, to remove dog hair from his suit trousers.

He didn't have a dog, but he did have an unexpected guest. When he'd leased the house, a large, energetic dust mop that he suspected was a Labrador-poodle mix had been making itself comfortable on the porch. The real estate agent had explained that the Caribbean had a serious problem with strays, and had offered to call animal control. But Theo had a soft spot for dogs, and this one was friendly. And there was something about the dog's thin frame that touched his heart. The dog needed to get its strength back, just like him. He'd taken to feeding it each morning, although he wouldn't let it into the house. As much as Theo was determined to make his life on St. Victoria work, he didn't want the dog to get too attached if he had to leave.

The dog had no such reservations. His enthusiastic greetings had left Theo's one good pair of trousers covered with fur.

Theo wanted to look presentable for his dinner with Willow, but so far, his attempts were not going well. His once wavy hair still stuck out at odd angles around his head. Except, of course, for the persistent spray that seemed to insist on falling directly over his forehead and into his eyes, no matter what he tried to do with it.

He told himself that there was no reason to be so nervous. It wasn't as though he was getting ready for a date. He was glad he'd clarified that with Willow from the start, although he still cringed at the awkward way his words had come out.

She'd lost no time in making certain that their dinner was not a date. He knew she'd been wise to do so, and he'd kicked himself for suggesting dinner in the first place. Why not lunch? Why not a coffee after work? Either of those would have accomplished his goal of getting to know Willow better, thereby bringing him that much closer to getting to know Maisie.

But his words—*What are the odds that you'll have dinner with me?*—had spilled out before he'd had time to think of something that might sound less like a date.

His feelings, especially his unspoken attraction to Willow, had betrayed him. He couldn't think of a worse idea than becoming romantically involved with Willow. His relationship with Maisie was completely at her discretion. After years of not knowing if he'd ever see his daughter, he couldn't allow anything to put his chance to get to know her at risk. Which meant that he had to ignore what he might feel for Willow. He'd already spent the first years of his daughter's life without her. If he and Willow were involved, and things became complicated, he couldn't risk losing Maisie again.

He wondered if things could have been different if he and Willow had met under more normal circumstances. He couldn't deny that he was physically attracted to Willow. He was entranced by the way the waves of her dark brown hair fell against the curve of her neck. And she held herself with such presence: though she had a petite frame, she projected a quiet authority that he imagined she'd developed over her years as a nurse. But it was her warmth, more than anything, that had led him to feel more attracted to her than to anyone he'd met in years. Granted, he'd gone on a very scant handful of dates since his illness was diagnosed four years ago. But even before the diagnosis, he couldn't remember being so struck by any woman's warmth and gentleness. Even back in her kitchen, when she'd been in the middle of explaining that she wasn't certain if he could see his own daughter, she'd expressed such genuine compassion. There was so much he wanted to know about Willow. He wanted to learn where that compassion came from, and who else in her life she might turn that compassion toward. From what he could tell so far, she shared it with everyone.

He was afraid that the more he got to know

Willow, the more certain he would be that he wanted her in his life. And no matter how much he wanted her, Maisie was the priority. Even if Willow felt something for him—and he didn't think she did—but even if she was as interested in him as he was in her, he was certain she would agree that their daughter had to come first.

He caught a glance of himself in the mirror as he threw on a crisp, white shirt and did up the buttons. He'd always been on the muscular side, but now his body looked positively gaunt, the missing muscle all too evident after years of treatment. Pale skin, uncontrollable hair. It felt like a cancer survivor's body, but it didn't feel like *his* body.

He wished it didn't feel as though there was so much riding on this dinner. He reminded himself, for what felt like the millionth time, that this wasn't a date. And yet the nervous feelings he had were so similar to the worries he typically had before a date. What if he couldn't think of anything to say? What if she hated the restaurant he'd picked? What if she decided she hated him, and he never got to know Maisie?

Stop panicking, he told himself firmly. *You got through cancer. You can get through this.*

* * *

He still hadn't returned his doctor's message from when he'd first arrived on the island. He'd been too nervous thinking about his upcoming dinner with Willow to spare a thought for checking in with his doctor. And he wanted some time to enjoy being in remission, before getting into a routine with his follow-up appointments. He needed to live his life. Which, at this moment, meant screwing up his courage and heading to the French Indian fusion restaurant in Williamtown where he was meeting Willow.

He took a deep breath and stepped out onto the veranda. The dog padded toward Theo with hopeful eyes, and leaned against his legs.

"I suppose a little more fur can't make a difference now," said Theo, scratching behind the dog's ears. "Wish me luck, old fellow."

In response, the dog thumped his tail twice on the porch. Theo decided to interpret this as a good sign. He was going to need all the help he could get.

Willow couldn't remember the last time she'd felt so nervous. Her mouth was dry, and as she sat across from Theo and tried desperately to think of something to say, it was all she could do to keep her hands from shaking.

Relax, it's not a date, she tried to tell herself. But somehow, it had the feeling of one.

Theo looked perfectly comfortable in his white, button-down shirt, while she'd simply thrown on an old sundress with a light shawl. But even on an un-date, as she referred to it in her mind, it was horribly awkward trying to think of something to say. She couldn't imagine how they would begin to feel comfortable with each other.

It didn't help that his hair, once again, fell just over his forehead. *Just try not to look at his hair, and control yourself*, she thought. It might have been a while since she'd had an evening out with another adult, but she had a feeling running her fingers through Theo's tousled hair in the middle of a crowded restaurant wouldn't do anything to reduce the awkwardness she felt.

When she'd first met Theo, his smile had caught her attention. Later, she'd found that she was quite taken with his eyes. But now, as she watched him peruse the menu, she realized that his hands were quite slender. Steady, careful hands.

Dammit, she thought. Was there anything about him that wasn't attractive?

She racked her brain for something besides

his appearance to talk about. *Work. Ask him how work is going.*

It was difficult, because she felt as though her mouth was full of cotton, but she managed to squeak out, "How are you adjusting to the clinic?"

He seized upon the question with an eagerness that made Willow suspect that he'd probably been searching for something to talk about, as well.

"It's fascinating. Although I'm not sure I'll ever get used to working with celebrity patients. I have to admit that it's not exactly the clientele I'd always imagined working with."

"Well, you've made quite an impression on Roni Santiago. Providing health care to the rich and famous might just be your calling."

"Perhaps. I suppose life is full of surprises. Speaking of which…sorry, again, for taking a job at your workplace. I never meant to make you uncomfortable."

She shrugged. "Don't worry. It was a surprise at first, but I should have anticipated it. There aren't too many options for oncologists on one small island."

He seemed to relax a bit at her words. "I'm glad you feel that way, because I think I might really like working at the Island Clinic. With so many unexpected changes, it hasn't always been easy to move forward with my career."

She realized that he was referring to the cancer. "I'm sure it couldn't have been easy to hold down a job consistently while you were ill."

"It wasn't. It's why I've mostly been in research positions, even though my passion is working directly with patients. One of the best things about the Island Clinic is that I get to do some clinical work on the side."

"You couldn't find something like that in England?"

"Oh, I could. But then, you see, I learned that my daughter had moved here. Finding her was the priority."

His jaw had that determined set to it again. Willow felt a twinge of guilt at having treated him with such suspicion at first. She didn't trust him yet. But she found that she wanted to.

"Is it hard to live so far from the rest of your family?" he asked.

"There's no other family. My parents died when I was very young, so I was raised by my grandmother, who passed away just after Maisie was born."

"I'm so sorry."

"It's all right."

He gave her a rueful smile. "Now there's a phrase I know all too well. Along with 'It's fine' and 'Don't worry about it.' That's my set of typical stock phrases for when someone asks a big question without realizing it, and then tries to apologize."

"Does that happen often?"

"Speaking as a cancer patient, it happens all the time. Sometimes all people can say is 'I'm so sorry,' and then all you can say back is 'It's all right.'"

She thought about that for a moment. Her response to Theo's question had been automatic. He was right; it was what she almost always said when people found out about her parents. And she was certain it was what he usually said when people learned he'd had cancer.

"I suppose I've been an orphan for so long that it just doesn't feel unusual to me," she said. "My parents died in a car accident before I was even a year old. Growing up, I did often wonder what they were like. I was lucky that I at least had Gran to tell me about them. But then, I always felt lucky to have Gran."

"So she was there to fill their shoes."

"In a way. She didn't replace them. She'd have been the first to admit that she never could have taken their place. But she made me feel loved enough that our tiny family felt much bigger than it actually was."

She hadn't expected to open up this much

to Theo. But she found that she enjoyed talking to him. No one had asked much about her family, or about Gran in particular, for years.

She couldn't help thinking about the parallels of her own life to Maisie's. Her daughter had only one other person in the world to rely on, just as Willow had, growing up. As a child, Willow had missed having the presence, the advice, of a father at times. As a mother, she often wished she had the ability to give Maisie a large family. In addition to enriching Maisie's life, it would have brought Willow peace of mind to know that Maisie would have other family if anything happened to Willow. She wondered if Maisie would begin to wish for more family as she grew older, just as Willow had.

Willow was sure Theo couldn't have known that her thoughts would turn in this direction when he'd asked about her family.

"What about you?" she asked. "Do you have much family back in England?"

"Four siblings, one of them a twin sister." He launched into a detailed description of the advantages and drawbacks of having a large family. In addition to his siblings, he seemed to have an extensive network of aunts, uncles and cousins who were all very involved in one another's lives. As they spoke, Willow realized that she was growing more comfortable. It had been so long since she'd spent an evening with another adult that she'd forgotten it could actually be fun.

But just as she was starting to relax and enjoy herself, a crash came from a few tables away. An older man was at the center of the commotion, surrounded by concerned waitstaff and restaurant patrons. Willow heard a faint cry of "Is anyone a doctor?"

"Looks like we're on call tonight," Theo said.

They approached the man, who was heavyset and seemed to be in his late sixties. His skin was beet-red, and his breathing was shallow and rapid. His forehead was hot to the touch, and his heart rate was elevated. He was conscious, but his words weren't making sense.

"He could be having a stroke," Theo muttered into her ear. A woman—presumably the man's wife—fluttered frantically about him in tears. "Does he have any neurological issues?" he asked her.

Willow turned to a waiter. "Get me a large pitcher of ice water," she said, ignoring Theo's quizzical look.

The man was wearing a heavy wool sweater, far too thick for the weather. "Help me get this off him," she said to Theo.

"It was a birthday present," the man's wife said through her tears. "He wanted to wear it even though I told him it was far too hot."

"Has he had any heavy exertion today?" Willow asked.

"We played tennis for a few hours, then I gave him the sweater and we came down here for a few drinks."

"How much alcohol has he had?"

"Two, maybe three drinks."

Willow nodded. "He's overheated. Don't worry—heatstroke can make people crash hard, but recovery is quick if we act fast." In fact, the man had already begun to come around as she rubbed his neck and forehead with ice.

"Drink this," she told him, lifting his head so he could sip a glass of cold water. "And no more alcohol for you today. Overexertion plus alcohol is a recipe for heatstroke."

Someone had called the paramedics, and the man was already sitting up on his own by the time they arrived on the scene.

"Will he be all right?" his wife asked.

"I'm sure he'll be fine," said Willow. "But he should go to the hospital to get checked out."

The woman thanked them profusely and proceeded to berate her husband. "I *told* you to take it easy," she scolded as she packed herself into the back of the ambulance with him.

"I'm impressed," Theo said. "I never thought of something as simple as heatstroke. I was thinking it was some sort of neurological condition. But then, I tend to overthink things."

"As a good researcher should," she said, smiling. "I've seen heatstroke a hundred times since moving to the island. Tourists aren't prepared for the heat of the Caribbean and don't realize how quickly they can overexert themselves."

As they headed back to their cold entrees, a waiter approached and let them know the cost of their meal had been compensated, to thank them for their help with the medical emergency. Willow thanked the waiter as Theo poked at his cold food.

"It's very kind of them, but I'm afraid this evening is a bit of a bust, isn't it?" said Theo. "Why don't we take a walk outside?"

They headed out to the boardwalk along the beach, where the sun was just beginning to set, illuminating the beach in tones of red and gold.

"I know this might sound strange, but I'm almost grateful for the medical emergency," Willow said. "It was nice to feel competent for a moment, after getting so nervous about our dinner together." She was careful to avoid the word *date*, even though, somehow, it was starting to feel like one.

"You were nervous? I would never have guessed."

She laughed. "Come on, you must have noticed how hard it was for me to talk at first."

"Maybe I didn't notice because I was nervous, too."

They stopped walking, and he gazed at her intently. She felt an unexpected wave of heat wash over her, a flush that had nothing to do with the warmth of the Caribbean air.

It's time to go home, she thought to herself. *Time to wrap that shawl around your shoulders like a respectable woman, and go home to take care of your child.*

But then Theo traced her arm, lightly, and her shawl slipped even lower on her shoulders. And somehow, Willow found herself not moving to put it back where it belonged. He was standing close to her, and she took in just how very tall he was. Her head fit just under his chin.

"How's your arm?" he said. For a moment she didn't know what he meant, but then she realized he was referring to when the reporter had grabbed her.

"Oh," she said distractedly. "It's fine. It's nothing…it barely left a mark."

The determined set to his jaw was starting to become familiar. She felt one of his arms circle her, protectively, and she didn't resist as he pulled her close against his chest.

She turned her face up toward his and lost herself in his clear, hazel eyes. He bent his head to hers and kissed her, softly at first, but then more deeply as she let her body melt against his. Things were moving far too fast, she knew, but she was also powerless to resist the sensation of his lips on hers. His arms enveloped her, one tight around her waist, the other caressing the waves of her hair that fell against her shoulder.

A current of heat ran through her entire body. It was agonizing to pull away from him, but she made herself do it. Not because she wanted the kiss to stop, but because she knew she'd reached the end of her resistance. If she didn't stop now, she never would. And there were so many reasons to stop. The primary reason was at home with Mrs. Jean, waiting for Willow to return and read her a bedtime story.

Theo held her for a moment longer, until she forced herself to step out of his arms.

The sun had gone down, and they were shrouded in darkness. There were only a few lights from further up the beach. After they'd walked together for a moment or two, Theo broke their silence.

"I'd give anything to know what you're thinking."

She wasn't sure how to begin. Or where to begin. She wanted to explain to him that she had sworn off relationships. She had responsibilities. She couldn't risk getting hurt again. And there was Maisie. She wanted him to understand.

But more than anything, she wanted him to kiss her again.

She was about to say that they'd made a mistake, but then she stopped. Honesty was important to her. "That was nice," she admitted.

His eyes were afire. "I can show you more than nice."

She was willing to bet that he could. But she had a daughter. She had to be cautious.

"I think, for now, we might have to leave it at nice," she said firmly.

"Because of the reason I think you're thinking of?"

"That's probably the main reason, yes."

He nodded. "Because no matter what we might be feeling for one another, those feelings have to be put on hold. We can't risk whatever happens between us affecting Maisie. Because that's the right thing to do."

She gave him the smallest of smiles. "I think you're starting to understand what it means to be a parent, Theo Moore."

He let out a long breath. "I think so, too. So nothing can happen between us."

She knew she should leave it at that. She should go home, without saying one thing more. She knew enough of who Theo was by now to know that if she never said another word about it, he would never bring up any of this again, out of respect for her.

But she couldn't accept that she'd had her last kiss with him.

She couldn't help herself. She blurted out, "Not for now, anyway."

He'd been looking out at the ocean, and now he whirled toward her. *Dammit.* His eyes did light up when he smiled. "Wait a minute. When you say, 'for now'…does that mean that there could be a *later* in our future?"

"I can't pretend to know what the future holds. But I think I can safely say that there could be a 'later' for us. And when that *later* time comes, I might be interested in more."

He smiled, and she was glad it was dark, so that he couldn't see her resistance melting away. "I can handle later," he said. "I've been waiting a long time for my life to start. I can wait a little more."

CHAPTER FIVE

"EVERYTHING LOOKS GOOD," said Willow, flipping Roni's chart closed. "Your prognosis is looking very strong, despite what the tabloids might say. I'll come back to start your next round of chemo in a few hours. Until then, keep resting, and let me know if you have any pain."

Roni scratched her French bulldog behind the ears. "I know the drill. I think Buttons and I will head up to the rooftop patio for some rest and relaxation in a few minutes. Then we'll take a little pre-chemo nap up there in the sun, so that we'll be well-rested for our post-chemo siesta this afternoon."

Willow smiled. "You've got the idea. The more you rest, the better your body is able to recover."

"Sounds logical enough, but I can't get used to all of this lying around. I need to work. I can't remember the last time I had so much time off. At least by doing chemo here, I can make it feel like a proper vacation." She fixed Willow with an eye. "Any chance you can have someone send up a mai tai while I'm on the roof?"

"If you like, but it'll have to be virgin. You know you shouldn't drink right now."

"Honey, I don't even want the alcohol. I just want to hold one of those big tropical drinks for the *effect*. I want to lean back on one of those lounge chairs and sip on something delicious, something decorated with tiny umbrellas and twenty different pieces of fruit and a flower or two."

"I'll put a note in to the kitchen and ask them to send up something ostentatious."

"That would be lovely. I want a drink that says, 'Screw you, cancer, I'm still living my life.'" Her expression grew sober. "That's the point, you know. Some of my friends thought that I should keep doing my treatment at home. I told them I needed more privacy, but that's not all it was about. This might sound silly, but I wanted to *show* cancer it hadn't beaten me. And I thought that if I could pretend that I was here by choice, as though I were on some sort of vacation, then no matter what happens with my treatment… I still win."

Willow impulsively reached out for Roni's

hand. "There's nothing silly about that. Maintaining a positive attitude is crucial for treatment."

Roni gave Willow's hand a little squeeze. "I'm glad you understand. It's not denial. I'm perfectly aware of my situation. It's just my way of coping, and it helps to be in a setting where everyone's agreed to play along." She traced her bulldog's ears. "Having a little company doesn't hurt, either. Back home, they wouldn't let me keep Buttons next to me during treatment."

"Technically, we don't allow it, either, so make sure to keep him under that sheet." According to clinic rules, the dog was supposed to stay in Roni's suite, but Willow had agreed to overlook his presence. Roni was so attached to the dog, and he clearly helped to lift her spirits.

Willow's initial reluctance to oversee Roni's care had quickly melted away as they got to know each other. Willow had been relieved to find that Roni was just as down-to-earth as she came across on television.

In fact, the most complicated part about working with Roni had nothing to do with Roni at all. It was Theo.

Several days had passed since their un-date. And their kiss.

The kiss was a problem, because it had been perfect.

The way his arms had enveloped her, holding her close to him. He was tall enough so that her head fit just under his chin, and when he'd bent his head to hers, she'd felt an excitement she thought she'd forgotten after all those years of having sworn off romance.

She'd felt very safe, very protected, in his arms. But the problem was that it wasn't safe at all. Kissing Theo, trusting Theo, *feeling* things for Theo…all of it put her in a very vulnerable position.

She might feel safe with Theo, but she couldn't trust her feelings. She'd felt safe with Jamie for years. And all that time, he hadn't really been himself with her. She'd nearly lost her dream of having a child because of his inability to tell her the truth about what he really wanted.

And now there was so much more at stake. Not just her own happiness, but Maisie's, too. One of the main reasons she'd sworn off relationships, aside from her own heartbreak, was her fear that Maisie could become attached to someone, and could be confused or even hurt if things didn't work out. But what if things didn't work out between Willow and a man who happened to be Maisie's father? She couldn't put her daughter through that.

She wanted to believe that she could trust Theo to protect her heart as much as she could trust him to protect her child. In the short time she'd known him, she'd noticed that he had a knack for saying just the right thing. But how could she trust that he was sincere? She'd already been with one man who'd said what she wanted to hear, rather than telling her the truth.

And so the kiss was a problem. Because no matter how perfect it had been, it didn't change the host of other issues she had to worry about. In fact, the more she thought about it, the more she became convinced that the kiss was a problem *because* it had been so perfect. If it had been a bad kiss, she could have forgotten about it by now and moved on.

Instead, it seemed determined to linger in her memory.

"Hey. Earth to Willow." Roni's voice brought Willow back to the present with a start.

"Oh, sorry. I must have spaced out for a minute. Let me just take a quick look at your lab results." She picked up Roni's chart.

"You just did that a few minutes ago, remember?"

Willow blushed, flustered. She *never* got distracted at work like this. "You're right. I don't know where my head is today."

"Maybe you were daydreaming about that hot date you had a few days ago."

Willow's eyebrows shot up her forehead. "You know about that?" Her chest began to tighten. Who else knew? Was it all over the clinic? "It wasn't exactly a date."

"Of course I know about it. Theo checks in on me every day. No, don't look like that," she said, noting Willow's affronted expression. "He didn't say a word to me about it. I heard him ask you to dinner the day I got here. I may have been feverish, but the two of you were just outside the door. Come on, dish. What's he like?"

At least there weren't rumors flying all over the clinic about the two of them. "It's...complicated."

Roni rolled her eyes. "Isn't it always."

"No, I mean it's really complicated. Theo is working here under a rather unusual set of circumstances, and even though I like him–"

Roni's gaze met hers. "You like him."

"Well, everyone seems to like him, so far."

"But not the way you do."

Willow was beginning to see how Roni had always got the guests on her show to open up so quickly about their most personal issues. The woman was relentless. "Theo and I are in a very unusual situation. Surely you'd rather rest than hear all the details," she protested weakly.

Roni chuckled. "I've got nothing but time to fill, and I need a good distraction. Besides, you can't leave me in suspense after all this talk about 'complications' and 'unusual situations.' What's the story with you and Dr. Moore?"

Willow was about to demur, but Roni's eyes seemed to plead for excitement. Suddenly, she realized that Roni might be the perfect person to talk to. She couldn't tell any of her friends from work because *they* all worked with Theo, too, and revealing her connection with him could create the very kinds of problems she wanted to avoid. And her friends outside of work were so eager to set her up with someone that they would probably ignore all of the problems that her feelings for Theo entailed. Roni was the perfect neutral party, and Willow had a feeling that she could trust Roni not to contribute to any gossip.

She took a deep breath. "You see, about four years ago, I decided to have a child on my own. But there was this mix-up." She went on to explain everything about the confusion at the clinic. She'd meant to just stick to the facts, but as she talked to Roni, she found herself opening up more and more about how conflicted her feelings were. Even though she didn't necessarily agree with the decision Theo had made to stay out of Maisie's life, given his circumstances, she could understand why he'd made the choice he did. She felt that after all he'd been through, he deserved to have a chance to get to know Maisie, especially as she was starting to believe he was serious about making a life on St. Victoria. But she also felt that she was putting Maisie's happiness at risk.

"That's the real problem, isn't it?" said Roni. "This isn't just about letting him get to know his child. I think you're afraid of him getting to know *you*."

Willow blushed again. "I don't know what to do. For the past three years, everything in my life has been about what's best for Maisie. I can't change that just because of an attraction to someone I barely even know."

"Even if that someone happens to be the father of your child?"

"*Especially* because of that. What if it doesn't work out? Where does that leave Maisie?"

"I hear you. But here's a thought—what if it does?"

Willow hesitated. "That's the other problem. I want to trust him, but I still don't know if I can. I'll admit that there's a lot I like about him. But…he ignored his daughter for three years. Supposedly, he's always wanted children, but if that were true, then shouldn't he have made every effort to be in her life when he had the chance?"

"Cancer, though," said Roni. "It's a hell of a mitigating circumstance."

"I know. And I want to be sympathetic to his situation, I really do. Except all these warning bells keep going off in my mind, telling me to be on my guard. But then, when we kissed, it felt so right." She clapped a hand over her mouth. She hadn't meant to tell Roni about the kiss.

But the look Roni gave her was full of understanding. "You've been hurt before, haven't you?" she said.

Willow nodded. Tears welled to her eyes, and she hastened to wipe them away.

"Then there's your answer," Roni said. "You don't have man problems. You have trust problems."

"What?"

"Please. I didn't host the highest-rated talk show in the world for fourteen years just to not be able to tell when someone's hiding from themselves. Your problem isn't with Theo at all."

"Of course it is. If he hadn't shown up here, I wouldn't have to be dealing with any of this."

Roni waved her hand in dismissal. "That's

just details. Date him, don't date him, it's your call. Although I have to admit that I'm biased toward you dating him. He did save my life, after all."

Willow couldn't disagree with the latter part of Roni's statement. However she might feel about Theo, his abilities as an oncologist were clear.

"My point is that he's not the cause of your problems. It's the memories of this person who hurt you, not Theo."

Willow wasn't sure she agreed. None of the turmoil she'd experienced lately had started until Theo had shown up. She'd never once questioned her decision to swear off relationships until Theo had started flashing that warm smile of his in her direction.

"But how can this not be about him?" she said. "He's the one who decided to show up here. He's the one who got a job at the same clinic I'm working at."

"Maybe he doesn't want to waste any more time. Look, I don't know what happened to you before, but I can say that cancer gives you a different outlook. You start looking at life differently, see all the opportunities you didn't take."

"Wait, Roni Santiago is talking about roads

not taken? Surely you can't have any regrets in life. Everyone in the world knows your name."

"There's more to life than just career. I'm talking about roads not taken in relationships. Opportunities of the heart. Maybe this Theo Moore is thinking of missed opportunities, too."

Maybe Roni had a point.

"So you think I should give him a chance?"

"Oh, no," Roni said, to Willow's surprise. "I think you should give *yourself* a chance. I think you should try to let go of the memories of whoever hurt you, if you can. And if, while you were doing that, you happened to also let yourself see where things might go with Theo…who knows? You might even have some fun. He's pretty easy on the eyes, after all. A little on the pale side. Needs some building up. But nice to look at overall. If I absolutely have to go through cancer, it doesn't hurt to have a handsome doctor to get me through it."

Willow pretended to look scandalized.

"Hey, I'm allowed to make the best of a bad situation."

Willow snorted. "I'll admit that it's not a *great* situation, but it's certainly not as bad as the tabloids say." She stood up from Roni's bedside and turned to leave. As she reached the door, she looked back and said, "Roni…

I'd appreciate it if you didn't tell anyone about our conversation."

Roni motioned to Buttons and said, "If you can keep my secrets, I can keep yours."

"Theo? Do you have an update on the Santiago case?" Nate's voice cut through Theo's reverie.

Theo pulled his attention back to the meeting. He was in a case conference with the clinic's senior staff members, reviewing updates on pressing clinical issues. His mind, though, kept drifting back to the kiss he'd shared with Willow several days ago.

But pleasant as it might be to reminisce, those thoughts weren't going to help him make a good impression at his new job. This was his first chance at a clinical position after he'd entered remission, and he wanted to shine. He forced himself to focus.

"Roni's prognosis is very good. She's had quality care before she arrived, and the plan is to continue her chemo regimen here. She has about two months left of her full course, at which time we'll reevaluate and update her treatment plan accordingly."

"Sounds like things are going smoothly," Nate replied. "Moving on—"

"There is a problem, though," Theo continued.

"With her treatment?"

"No. With the press." Theo threw a tabloid paper onto the conference table. Its headline read Roni Santiago Fights Mysterious Deadly Illness! "For one thing, these headlines are wildly misleading. It seems like in the absence of any real information they're just making things up."

"Nothing we can do about that," Nate replied. "We can't reveal any confidential information about our patients, and Roni wants utter privacy."

"That's not all, though. The press corps camped outside the clinic has been pushy and aggressive since the day they arrived. I'm worried about how they're responding to staff. One of them already grabbed Willow's arm when she tried to walk away from him." Theo felt a twinge of guilt, as Willow had said there was no need to mention the incident to Nate. Still, seeing the throng of press outside when he arrived at work every day was unsettling. They seemed to be constantly pushing back against the security staff.

"Is Willow all right?"

"She's fine. But I'm concerned that things could have been more serious. I've never seen reporters act in such a way."

"It's because it's not just press, it's paparazzi," another doctor chimed in. "They'll do anything to get a compromising photo of Roni. Theo's right, though. We should do something about it before the situation escalates."

Nate nodded. "I'll talk to the clinic security staff about ways we might need to change procedure. Everyone should feel safe coming here, no matter what. But don't worry, Theo. We've dealt with these kinds of situations before."

"Yes, I heard about the K-pop band," Theo said, and everyone laughed.

"*That* was a fiasco," said Nate. "I think every single teenage girl on the island faked an illness or injury in order to come here and catch a glimpse of those boys."

Most of the doctors were still laughing as they left the conference room. Theo was glad that he seemed to be fitting in well. But as he headed back toward his office, he found himself wishing that he knew where he stood with Willow.

They'd had ample opportunity to see each other over the past few days, as they were both part of Roni Santiago's medical team. She'd been warm, but professional, and he'd tried his best to respond in kind. He always seemed to find himself tongue-tied around her.

Though, for some reason, he hadn't felt nervous at all during their kiss. It had seemed like the most natural thing in the world to bend his head to hers and to feel her mouth yield to his, with nothing but the gentle lapping of the waves on the beach to keep him from getting utterly lost in the moment, in *her*.

He understood why she'd pulled back from him. If he knew one thing about Willow, it was that she was protective of her daughter. There was no way for the two of them to become involved without acknowledging the fact that it could be confusing for Maisie. He hoped Willow knew that he'd agreed with everything she'd said about wanting to put their feelings on hold because of Maisie. He thought it was for the best, too. Complicating, or even losing, his chance to get to know Maisie was out of the question. But losing the chance to kiss Willow again…well, that was also a grim prospect.

After she'd pulled away from their kiss, he'd thought, for a moment, that Willow would say that they had no chance at all. But he'd been relieved that she'd kept the door open for… something.

He wasn't sure what that something might be, or just how far into the future she envisioned "later" to be. He was still trying to think of a way to bring it up with her when he arrived at his office and found a sticky note stuck to his computer screen. It was from Willow, inviting him to meet her for lunch in the cafeteria.

He arrived to find her already nibbling at a chocolate croissant.

"Interesting choice," he said, sitting across from her. "A cafeteria staffed by Michelin-star-quality cooks, and yet you're opting for a coffee and croissant for lunch."

She closed her eyes in pleasure as she took a bite. "Clearly you haven't yet enjoyed the magic of the Island Clinic morning pastry table. There are hardly any leftovers by lunch, but I managed to snag this one today."

"I'll have to try one soon."

She gave him a mock glare and pulled the croissant toward herself. "Don't get any ideas. This one's mine."

He held up his hands. "Your croissants are safe with me."

She took a long sip of coffee, and he had a feeling she was gathering her thoughts. He was bracing himself for whatever she might say next. He hoped, more than anything, that she wasn't about to tell him that they couldn't see each other, because of Maisie. And yet if she was, well, then…he might not like it, but he could understand.

"I really enjoyed having dinner with you," she said. He noticed that she seemed as careful to avoid the word *date* as he was. "It was my first night out in a long time, and it was fun."

"Even with the medical emergency?"

"Especially with that. It gave me a chance to show off a little."

He sighed. "I can't help but feel that there's a 'but' coming."

"Theo, honesty is extremely important to me. Which is why I want to tell you that I had a good time the other night. And... I am enjoying getting to know you. I've been thinking a lot about roads not taken, and if it were just me, if I were completely on my own, then this would probably be a road I'd want to explore. But I'm not on my own."

He reached across the table and covered her hand with his, and she didn't move away. "I appreciate your honesty, and I understand. And just so you know, you're not in this alone. Protecting Maisie is important to me, too."

"I can see that. And that's why we need to take things really, really slowly."

His world stopped for a minute. He wasn't sure he'd heard correctly. Once again, he'd been so certain that Willow was going to tell him that she couldn't be romantically involved with him at all. But if she were talking about taking things slowly, then that meant he had a chance.

"We need to take our time," she continued. "We've both been through some very sudden changes lately, and we need some time to adapt. If it were just me, I might be ready to jump in with both feet. But I don't want to throw lots of sudden changes Maisie's way."

Her hand was still under his, on the table. Cautiously, without breaking eye contact, he turned his hand so that he was holding hers. "So just to be clear, this isn't a full stop, but a slowdown."

She held his hand as firmly as she held his gaze. "I need you to be okay with slow."

He couldn't stop the relieved grin that broke over his face. "Are you kidding me? I am *thrilled* with slow. If slow is my chance to get to know my daughter, and you, then slow is my new favorite speed."

She gave his hand a squeeze before she took hers back. "I hope you can understand."

"Willow, I do. I meant it when I said that you're not in this alone. Protecting Maisie will always be my first priority."

She nodded, but he wasn't sure if she understood what he meant. How could she? He hadn't yet had a chance to explain to her what having children meant to him.

"When I was diagnosed with cancer, I worried that having lots of children would be one

of many dreams that I'd have to put on hold.
I didn't know if it was ever going to happen.
Having my sperm frozen was my last chance.
But even with that, there was no way to be sure
that I would ever have children. All it did was
help to increase my chances a little. And so
when the clinic had their accident and Maisie
was conceived…to me, it wasn't an accident. It
was a miracle. And even though I don't know
her, she's very precious to me, because she
represents part of a dream I once had. There's
nothing I wouldn't do for her. Including taking things slow."

Willow was staring at him intently. Theo
hoped his words had made sense. He hoped he
hadn't come on too strong, but even if he had,
he didn't think he could have put it any other
way. He'd meant every word.

But then she smiled. "I know a little something about feeling like your dreams are being
taken away. Maisie represents a dream for me,
too."

He realized that she must be referring to the
reason she'd had Maisie via donor insemination. It was such a personal decision that he
hadn't yet had a chance to ask her about it, but
he was curious.

"What kind of dream did you have?" he
asked gently.

"Oh, nothing too uncommon, I suppose. I didn't grow up in a big family like yours. But I was always envious of people who did. I imagined having a large family of my own. And I thought my ex did, too. He'd said he did. Until, after eight years together, he decided he didn't."

Theo winced in sympathy. "It's an awfully big thing to change one's mind about."

"The worst part is, I could have forgiven him a long time ago if he'd simply changed his mind about it. But he always said that we'd have children someday, when the time was right."

"And the right time never came?"

She shook her head in frustration. "At first I was furious with him. All that time, he could have told me the truth, instead of saying the things he thought I wanted to hear. If he had, then maybe we could have parted as friends. Maybe we could have both found people who wanted the same things we did. But now I think I was just as angry with myself, for not seeing the truth sooner. Of course Jamie wouldn't want children. He didn't even *like* children. He never wanted to spend any time with his young nieces and nephews. He'd even complain if we went to a restaurant and there were children nearby."

"It sounds as though you two were rather badly matched."

"To say the least of it. I can see now that we weren't right for each other. But we started dating when we were very young. I'd never broken up with anyone before. And the worst part wasn't just losing the relationship. It was losing that whole dream of having a family."

"And so you decided to have Maisie."

"Exactly," she said. "So you see, Theo, I do know how it feels to worry that your dreams are slipping away."

Theo realized that he and Willow might be more similar than he'd thought. They'd both had to find creative ways around life's obstacles. He found his respect for her growing even more.

"I had so much of my future built up around Jamie, and so when we broke up, I knew that I never wanted to put myself through that pain again," she continued. "Especially once Maisie arrived. And so I swore off relationships for a while. I guess what I'm trying to say is that I'm pretty out of practice with…certain things."

He smiled. "So we go slow."

"Yes."

He tried not to let his expression betray his thoughts. *She* was out of practice? He hadn't been with anyone for nearly four years. His body was such a shadow of what it used to be after chemo that it was hard enough for him to look at it, let alone anyone else.

But when he'd kissed Willow on the boardwalk, his body had seemed to know just how to respond when he'd felt her hot skin against his, out of practice or not.

He wanted very much to find some secluded place with Willow now, where they could finish what they'd started on that boardwalk, and catch up on whatever practice they needed after taking the past few years off from relationships.

But they were trying to take things slow. And so instead, he said, "I found a house to rent last week. I decided to decline the staff housing here, in favor of increased privacy. Would it be going slow enough if I invited you and Maisie over to see the house this weekend? We could make it a bit of a housewarming party. I could spend some time with her, and you can see if the house meets with your approval."

"You have a house already? You've only been here three weeks."

"It turned out to be much easier to find a place to rent than I thought. It even came with a dog."

"I...didn't know that was typical."

"The landlord said he'd been living on the porch for months. He's very friendly. Do you like dogs? Does Maisie?"

"She'll be over the moon. She's been pestering me for one for ages, but I was going to wait for her birthday next year."

"You'll come, then? It's a…date?"

"It's a start."

CHAPTER SIX

THE HOUSE THEO had rented turned out to be on a stretch of beach just outside Williamtown, about a twenty-minute walk from Willow's home. Willow was grateful for the walk, as she wanted time to collect her thoughts. This would be the first time Maisie would have any amount of interaction with Theo, and she was nervous about how it would go.

Willow had simply told her that they were visiting a friend. The plan was to have a picnic lunch on the beach, and Maisie chattered excitedly from her stroller about the dog Willow had said would be there.

Maisie, Willow knew, would be fine, no matter how this afternoon went. After all, as far as she was concerned, this was just another day out. To Willow, it was much more. Her conversation with Roni had been spinning in her head all week. She knew that she hadn't had feelings like those she felt for Theo in a long time. But despite all the reasons *not* to start anything with Theo—and there were so many good reasons—maybe Roni was right. Maybe all of those reasons were nothing more than Willow's way of hiding from herself.

Swearing off relationships had let her feel safe. For years, she'd told herself that she could be content with just herself and her daughter. But then, she'd never encountered anyone like Theo over the past few years. Someone who gave rise to the first stirrings of a desire for something more.

Or perhaps "first stirrings" was a bit of an understatement. She still remembered the way Theo's hand had brushed her neck when they kissed. The way her shawl had dropped down from her shoulder.

She'd wanted so much more than just a kiss.

But she'd also meant what she'd said, about wanting to take things slow. The attraction she felt for him had disrupted her calm life and left her feeling thrown off-balance, because she knew the heartbreak that could come if things went badly.

She'd felt encouraged by the conversation they'd had in the cafeteria. But then, Theo always knew what to say. It was whether he followed his words up with actions that mattered.

They approached Theo's house, where he waved to them from the porch. Like their own house, it was built on stilts to protect against hurricanes. Maisie hopped out of her stroller and they traipsed down the narrow pathway, until Maisie came to a dead stop.

"No," she said.

"What is it, love?"

Maisie pointed a chubby finger. "No dog."

A large, curly-haired dog sat placidly next to Theo on the porch. As Willow and Maisie stared at it, it placed its head on Theo's knee and gazed at him with brazen adoration.

"This is Bixby," Theo said, scratching the dog behind its ears as Bixby closed his eyes in ecstasy. "He came with the house. He lives out here on the porch, and seems very determined to stay."

Maisie stepped back, and peeked out from behind Willow's skirt. "What's wrong, Mais?" Willow asked. "I thought you were excited to meet the doggy."

"That one's too big."

"He is a big fellow, isn't he?" said Theo, rubbing Bixby's sides. The dog stood up and shook, and Maisie cowered behind Willow even more. Willow guessed the dog was some mix of Labrador and poodle. He seemed to resemble the average dust mop, with about the same amount of coordination.

"Here's the great thing about big dogs, though," Theo continued. "They're big enough to hug, which is important when you've got a dog with as much fluff as Bixby here. And they're clever. Bixby and I have only known each other a few weeks, but he can do all kinds of tricks."

Maisie's lower lip began to pout, and Willow knew where this was going. "She doesn't have much experience with dogs," she said to Theo. "I think she was expecting a small puppy."

"He's very well-behaved," Theo said.

"Yes, I can see he's perfectly calm, but it's not him I'm worried about." She jerked her head toward Maisie, whose lower lip was now trembling. Willow was certain tears were on the horizon. Her protective instincts were on the alert. Bixby clearly wasn't a vicious animal—at the moment, he was trying to lick Theo's face—but she didn't want her daughter to feel afraid. "It might be best to take the dog inside," she said.

"Let's just try one thing more," Theo said. Willow grit her teeth. Theo might mean well, but he didn't seem to understand that Maisie was about to implode. He needed to take the dog inside before she had a full meltdown.

"Look at what he can do," Theo said. "Shake, Bixby." The dog sat up, alert, and extended his paw.

Willow began, "I don't think that's going to—" But to her surprise, Maisie had stuck her head out from behind her skirt.

"What else can he do?"

"Oh, lots of things. He can give me a high-five." Theo and Bixby demonstrated. "But *this* is my favorite. Let me show you."

Maisie watched intently as Theo showed her a tennis ball and three paper cups. Willow watched Maisie just as intently. Only a moment ago, her child had been showing classic signs of an imminent Maisie Meltdown, and Willow had been determined to rescue her from anything that could cause her a moment's fear. Now, she was taking tentative steps toward the porch, all traces of tears gone as she watched Theo and the dog.

Theo hid a tennis ball underneath one of the paper cups, and switched the placement of each cup in front of Bixby. "Go on, Bix. Find your ball."

The dog knocked over one paper cup, then another. Neither hid the ball. He placed his paw on the third cup and looked expectantly at Theo.

"Sorry, boy," Theo said. He turned the cup over to reveal that it, too, had been empty.

"You tricked him!" Maisie shouted. "Poor Bixby, that wasn't fair!"

Theo tossed the tennis ball to Maisie, who caught it with both hands. "Maybe you can be a better playmate for him. He loves fetch. He'll bring that ball back to you as many times as you're willing to throw it."

Minutes later, Maisie and Bixby were running back and forth together on the beach.

"I don't get it," Willow said, trying to wrap her head around what had just happened. "Look at her. One minute she's about to go into full-on tantrum mode, and now suddenly they're the best of friends."

"Well, Bixby's easy to make friends with."

"No, it's more than that. I was ready to jump in and protect her, even though she clearly didn't need it. But you gave her a chance to see that there was nothing to be afraid of."

"She just needed a little time to adjust to a new situation, that's all. Children sometimes think they're scared, when really, they just need a moment to get used to something new."

"How do you know so much about children?"

"I had a large family, remember? I spent my teenage years looking after my younger cousins. It taught me how to tell the difference between real tears and an attempt to escape a situation."

Theo had set up a picnic blanket on the beach where they could have lunch and watch Maisie play. As they filled their plates with grapes and cheese, Willow heard Maisie shriek with laughter from further down the beach.

It had always been important to her to be protective of Maisie, but she realized that her daughter did, indeed, need to be pushed to face her fears. If she'd had her way, Maisie would still be huddled behind her skirt, instead of running on the beach, playing with a dog. It was the swimming lessons all over again, only this time, someone had given Maisie a chance to be brave, instead of giving in at the first sign of a trembling lip.

"I know I should be firmer with her," she said to Theo. "I'm probably lucky that Maisie's well-behaved most of the time, because I'm not great at standing my ground with her. The first sign of tears, and I'm usually ready to give in."

"I'm sure it can't be easy, being a single parent. You've got no one to back you up, or reassure you that you're on the right track."

"Intellectually, I know it's not easy, but it's hard to remember to give myself a break. I chose this life, so I feel like I should be better at it. I should push her more. I want her to be brave and open to adventure."

"Didn't you push her by moving her out here in the first place? That was a bold and adventurous move."

"I suppose. But I think Maisie would have me wrapped around her little finger no matter where we lived."

"Was it a hard decision, to leave London?"

Willow shook her head emphatically. "No. It was a careful decision. It was a big change, but nothing about it was hard."

"Really? Surely there must have been some difficulty adjusting. You moved thousands of miles from everything you knew. And London has so much to offer a child. It must have been hard to take Maisie away from all those experiences."

"Hardly. Maisie was missing out on much more in London. She was always being watched by someone else, stuck at daycare or with a neighbor. I was so busy all the time, and yet on the salary I was making, I could barely make ends meet. I grew up in Islington, and it was all I knew. But Maisie deserved more. At the very least, she deserved to have her mother around."

"It must have been hard on you, too."

"I was missing so much of her life. And

then…" She paused, because it was still painful to think about, but she pressed onward, anyway. "I missed her first word."

"No!"

"Yes. She was about one year old, and the daycare workers mentioned that she'd been saying 'horsie' when she wanted her stuffed horse at naptime. They thought I already knew. Apparently she'd been saying it for weeks. I was so upset that I'd missed it. And sad, of course, that it wasn't 'Mummy,' although I suppose that's silly. Children say all kinds of different things for their first word. But I couldn't help feeling as though it meant something. That if I'd been around more, maybe her first word *would* have been 'Mummy,' and maybe she'd have said it to me."

"But you *were* there for her. Maybe you weren't physically with her as often as you wished you could be, but you were doing the best you could to support her."

"I was. But it wasn't what I wanted. And when I found the job here…well, that was the first time I started to hope that maybe I *could* have it all. I could support our family and spend lots of time with Maisie, too."

"And it…wasn't as though you had any family you were taking her away from."

"No. I mean, I'd assumed you didn't want

anything to do with her." She could see that her words caused him some pain, but it was the truth. And even though she didn't want to hurt him, it did mean something to her that he was feeling the weight of all that he'd missed. She touched Theo's arm lightly. "We can't change the past. I can't change that Maisie and I have built a life here, just as you can't change that you weren't able to be part of our lives for the past few years. What matters is what we want the future to look like."

"Speaking of the future, there's something I've been meaning to talk about. You don't have to make any big decisions about it yet, but I wanted you to know that there's lots of family in England, for Maisie, if she ever wants it. Some of my brothers and sisters have children. She has cousins her age, and grandparents who would be delighted to spoil her rotten."

The thought gave Willow pause. Somehow, she hadn't considered what Theo's large family might mean for Maisie. Since Maisie's birth, she'd envisioned life with just the two of them. But now Maisie had cousins. She didn't know what that would be like. She'd never had a cousin.

She recalled the brief surge of jealousy she'd felt when Theo first arrived on the island. The idea of her special bond with Maisie changing to include anyone else had been inconceivable. She'd just got used to the idea of Maisie spending any time with Theo. It felt strange to consider that there might be a whole host of other people who also wanted to be in Maisie's life.

"Do they know about her?"

"No. The only person I've ever told is my twin sister, Becca. She's very good about privacy. Telling the others would only complicate things."

"How so?"

"For one thing, most of my family members, whom I love dearly, are not the best with boundaries. Half of them would swarm into your life the moment they became aware of your existence. They're not big on personal space. It's their way of showing love, but it can be very overwhelming. I think it should be your choice whether they become part of Maisie's life or not."

Or Maisie's choice, she supposed, when Maisie got older. Willow thought of all the times that she had seen families support each other through difficult diagnoses and medical emergencies. She'd always been touched, and a little envious, when she saw family members come together through tough times. Willow was proud of her own independence, but there were many times when she wished she had more family to rely on for support. And even though she might not ever have the support she wished for, it might be possible for Maisie to have family members who would be there for her when she needed them. It brought a strange, bittersweet ache to her heart to think about it. As much as she wished she could meet Maisie's every need, she knew there were some shoes she could never fill.

Losing her own parents at an early age had taught her that lesson well. Gran had loved Willow with all her heart, but she'd never been able to give Willow the large family she'd longed for. And sometimes love wasn't enough. There had always been the danger that if something happened to Gran, Willow would be all alone. But Maisie wouldn't have to face that risk, with Theo and his family involved in her life. No matter what her daughter faced, she could have the family support that Willow had always longed for.

"Even if they're intrusive, it must have been comforting to have your family around you while you were going through cancer," she said. "They must be so glad you're finally in remission."

He looked away, and she thought she saw a guilty expression in his eyes. "What is it?"

"I may have somewhat downplayed my cancer to them. They never really knew how bad it was."

"How on earth would you do that? *Why* would you do that?"

"My father was diagnosed with Alzheimer's shortly before I started chemo. He's still doing all right, as far as his health goes, but his mind is very different from what it used to be. It's been heartbreaking for my mum. Watching her go through that, I knew I couldn't burden her with everything I was going through, too. So I downplayed everything. I emphasized the cure rate for melanoma, and I never mentioned my treatment unless someone asked about it. I hid the side effects from everyone, except Becca. I tried to act like I had more energy than I did, and I stayed away from everyone on the worst days."

She couldn't believe what she was hearing. Theo had something she'd wanted for her entire life: a family that could support him through tough times. And yet when he'd needed them most, he hadn't reached out to them at all.

"I'm surprised you could keep such a secret from your family, if they're as pushy as you say they are."

"It wasn't easy, believe me. But everyone was very upset about my father. I was determined not to burden them any further."

"With the truth? Don't you think they would have preferred to know what was going on?"

"I didn't lie to them."

"But you put on a facade. You told them what you thought they wanted to hear, rather than being honest with them."

She could see that he was uncomfortable with this interpretation of events. "I wanted to do what was best for them," he said. "I love my family. I couldn't bear to see what my mother was going through. She was just starting to realize that she was losing my father just a little bit more, every day. I couldn't stand to think that she'd have to worry about me, too."

She could see that his intentions came from a good place, but she worried that the results of his choices left people feeling shut out. For three years, she'd thought he hadn't cared about Maisie at all because of his silence. And even recently, when he'd arrived on St. Victoria, he'd been silent for that first week because he'd said he hadn't wanted to bother her, while she'd begun to think that he'd left the island and given up on fatherhood. She believed that Theo meant well, but she wondered if he realized that by keeping his feelings so far inside, he was shutting himself out from people who might care about him.

And if Theo was so used to shutting people

out, then would he shut her out? Or Maisie? She needed to know.

"What about now?" she said. "I hate to suggest this, but what if the cancer comes back? How can I know for sure that you're not just downplaying anything that's wrong so that I'll feel better?"

"That's not going to happen," he said.

"But how do I know?"

He thought for a long moment. "I suppose all I can do is promise to tell you if anything changes," he said.

"And will you?" she said. "You'll tell me at the first sign of any problems?"

"Yes. Only there aren't going to be any problems."

"How can you possibly say that? Surely you must worry about the cancer coming back. How could you not, as an oncologist *and* a recovering cancer patient."

"I worry about it sometimes, in an abstract way."

"No." She shook her head. "I don't believe you. You're scared about it, I can tell."

He raised his eyebrows. "Scared?"

"Absolutely. And it's completely understandable. Anyone in your situation would feel the same way. I even feel a little scared, thinking about your health."

"Willow, there's no need to worry. I'm fine."

She shook her head. "I don't need you to re-assure me that you're okay. I need you to be real with me about how you're feeling."

"And you believe I'm feeling scared."

"I know you are."

"How?"

She nodded toward where Bixby was running on the beach. "Because that poor dog lives on your front porch."

He looked more confused than ever. "Bixby? But he's happy there. I've bought him a bed, and toys."

"You've even taught him a few tricks. Anyone can see that you love that dog. So…why the porch, Theo? Why doesn't your dog live in the house?"

His shoulders slumped in defeat. He'd seen where she was going. "Because I don't want him to get too attached. He's just a dog. If anything happened to me, he couldn't understand. Who would take care of him if the cancer came back?"

They sat together for a while, watching Maisie play on the beach. After a long while, he said, "I suppose you're right. I am a little scared about the cancer coming back. But my prognosis is looking very good. There's really no reason to worry."

"Besides the fact that cancer is just generally a scary and worrisome thing?"

"Besides that, yes."

"Good."

He looked quizzical. *"Good?"*

"Yes. Not that your cancer could return. That's sad to think about, and I hope you don't ever have to face that. But we've just been talking about how you kept the extent of your illness hidden from the people closest to you, and I need to be able to trust that if you were dealing with something serious, you'd tell me. So I'm glad that you could finally admit that you're scared. Because the things that happen to you won't just affect you, they'll affect Maisie, too. So I need you to be open about what you're going through."

She wasn't sure how to put it into words, but Willow also knew that *she* would be extremely upset if anything were to happen to Theo. She didn't want to be taken by surprise, if possible. And more than that, she wanted to know that Theo wasn't the kind of person who shut other people out of his life during difficult times. The whole point of family, as she'd always seen it, was to support one another. She needed to know that Theo could be emotionally accessible. He might claim to distance himself in order to protect his loved ones, but she didn't think that was the whole story. He'd talked about his family having poor boundaries sometimes, and she wondered if he'd grown overly cautious about how much he allowed himself to depend on people.

Well, they certainly had that in common. But if Theo couldn't let a dog that he was clearly fond of into his own home, what did that say about his ability to get close to his child?

But Theo had promised to be open with her. And she did believe that he was sincere in his desire to protect those he cared about. She might not agree with his past choices, but it seemed that he was doing his best to change his future. After all, he was here now. And she was more than willing to give both Theo, and herself, a chance.

She allowed her body to relax into the crook of his arm, letting herself enjoy feeling him circling her, protecting her.

He buried his nose in her hair and murmured, "Think she'll notice if I steal a kiss?"

"Later," she murmured back.

Hours later, Willow had left, an exhausted Maisie asleep in her stroller.

Theo waited until Bixby had settled down on his porch bed, and then went inside to sink into an armchair.

He should have felt flushed with accomplishment. And in many ways, he did. The day had offered him exactly what he'd hoped to find when he came to St. Victoria. He'd spent time with Maisie and had found that even at just three years of age, his daughter had a personality all her own. She was funny and bright, fond of tickles and delighted to show him interesting objects she'd found on the beach. It had warmed his heart to find her so eager to connect with him, even though he and Willow had agreed that she wasn't old enough yet to understand who he was in relation to her.

But his joy was bittersweet. Getting to know Maisie had shown him the stark reality of all the things he'd missed by staying away from her for these past few years. Willow's voice had sounded so pained when she'd spoken of missing Maisie's first words. But he'd missed all of it. The more he spent time with her, the more he began to regret his choice to stay away from her. And from Willow. The most beautiful woman he'd ever met, the warmest, kindest woman he'd ever known, had been right there in London all along. All he'd had to do was call her.

But he couldn't have. Not then. Not while he was facing the worst of the cancer. If he couldn't bear the thought of burdening his family with an accurate picture of his illness, then he certainly couldn't have shared that information with the mother of his child.

He'd stayed away for their own good. But the cost of the choice he had made hit him harder today than it had in three years. It made his heart ache to think that Willow had struggled with her finances in London. He should have been there to help.

If he were faced with the same decision today, he wondered, would he still make the same choice he'd made more than three years ago? Now that he knew how much he cared for both of them, it would be far, far more difficult to stay out of their lives. At the time, he'd been so certain he was making the right choice, because he was doing it to protect them. But had it been the right choice? Suppose the worst happened, and he had to go through all of it again. Would it be better for him, to have Willow and Maisie there to support him? More importantly, he wondered if Willow was right; if it would be better for the two of them to know what he was going through.

He couldn't change the past. All he could do was move forward.

He glanced at his phone and felt a twinge of guilt. He'd promised Willow that he'd be open with her about the cancer. And so far, he had been. His doctors had all been extremely positive about his prognosis now that he was in remission. But he hadn't responded to a single message from any of his doctors since he'd arrived in the Caribbean a few weeks ago.

As a doctor, he knew his avoidance was foolish. The best thing he could do was call his medical team back immediately so that he could arrange to have oversight of his care transferred to doctors in St. Victoria. Still, he hesitated. For the first few days, he'd told himself he was busy, that he was waiting to get settled in, and that he'd call when he had the time. But now Theo's doctors were calling every day, and he was deleting their messages without listening to them first.

It wasn't that he was afraid of what those messages might say exactly. It was more that he simply wanted a break from being a patient. He wanted one part of his life that wasn't touched by cancer. He was enjoying the sense of finally, *finally* starting the life he wanted. He didn't have to schedule his work life around medical appointments. He was starting to connect with his daughter. And he might have a real chance at a relationship with Willow. He just wanted a moment to enjoy all of that, without the next medical appointment looming over his head.

But the moment was turning into days, which were turning into weeks. Soon, it would be months, and Theo would have to acknowledge that he wasn't just taking a break. He was hiding. And Willow had been right, on the beach: he was scared.

But he couldn't hide forever. It was time to call his doctor back. Not just for himself, but for the people he cared about. He wanted to keep the promise he'd made to Willow, and be honest with her.

He checked his watch. It would be just after eight p.m. in London if he called now. His doctor wouldn't be in the office, but he could leave a message. For a moment he wondered if he should wait until the next morning, so he could speak with his doctor directly. No, he thought, best to get it done now. Who knew how he might feel in the morning. If he waited any later to make the call, he might change his mind.

To his surprise, his doctor answered the phone. "Theo!" Dr. Raida greeted him. "Where have you been? I was getting worried."

Theo's heart sank. He liked his doctor, but until that moment, he hadn't realized how much he'd been hoping that Dr. Raida had gone home for the evening. He'd wanted to leave a quick message and then hang up, but hearing his doctor's voice brought back all the memories he'd been hoping to avoid.

"I'm sorry, Doc. I've been incredibly busy. As are you apparently, if you're working after eight p.m. tonight."

His doctor *tsked* over the phone. "I had a few emergencies this morning and decided to stay late to finish up with some paperwork—and a good thing, too, or I'd have missed your call. You of all people should know how important it is to keep close contact with your treatment team. What kind of oncologist drops off the face of the earth the moment he's in remission?"

"I noticed that you've been trying to get hold of me."

"Yes, and thank goodness I finally did. We need to do another biopsy."

Theo's stomach went cold. "What?"

"I'm sorry, Theo. I know that's not something you want to hear. But I was looking over some imaging from your case just before you left. You remember that skin lesion we took a picture of? I wasn't too worried about it at first, but I've talked it over with some colleagues, and we agreed that we should take a tissue sample to rule out cancer."

Theo held his forehead in his hands.

"This is just a precautionary measure. Just

to be on the safe side. Don't get too concerned yet. By all other indications, your prognosis is very good. But we want to be absolutely sure everything's okay."

"I can't leave the Caribbean right now." He tried to keep his voice from cracking.

"That's all right. Have you set up care with any doctors there?"

"Not yet. I'll get to work on that right away."

"Do that, please. We'll fax your records over as soon as we can and talk about coordinating care."

"Sure thing," Theo said as he hung up the phone.

Amid all the devastation, turmoil and fear that flooded his mind, one thought emerged, clear as day: he could not tell Willow about this.

Things were just starting to go well, both with her and with every other area of his life. He couldn't let cancer screw everything up again.

He remembered what he'd told her on the beach. And he remembered what she'd said about her ex, in the cafeteria. How he'd just told her what he thought she wanted to hear, instead of the truth.

But this was different. For one thing, nothing had really changed about his situation.

He didn't need to update Willow about anything, because there was nothing new to re-
port. Just because his doctor was ordering a
biopsy didn't mean that his remission status
had changed. There would be nothing new to
tell Willow until after he had the test results.
And why mention it before then? What if the
test results were clear, and he'd worried her
for no reason?

And another thing: he wasn't trying to de-
liberately mislead Willow. He just wanted to
protect her. The same way he'd tried to protect
his family from the full knowledge of what
he was facing. The way he'd tried to protect
Maisie from the loss of a parent. Willow might
say that she wanted him to be open with her
about what he was going through, but she probably didn't understand the magnitude of what
she was asking.

He'd start setting up appointments tomorrow, he decided. Not at the clinic, but at St.
Victoria Hospital. They might not have the resources of the Island Clinic, but they should
be perfectly capable of coordinating with his
care team in London. With no danger of the
information getting back to Willow.

CHAPTER SEVEN

OVER THE NEXT few weeks, Willow's life began to settle back into an easy routine of work, caring for Maisie and spending time with Theo. She realized that over her past year on St. Victoria, she'd never had any visitors, and it was fun to play tour guide and show Theo all that the island had to offer. For Maisie, that meant hours showing Theo her favorite dolls, her tea sets and her rather alarming collection of small dried crustacean bodies gleaned from the tide pools near their home. For Willow, it meant visiting various hiking spots and music venues on the island. Although neither of them said it outright, many of their outings felt suspiciously like *dates*, although Willow expected that, if pressed, she and Theo would both describe their time together as simply "getting to know each other."

Maisie became attached to Theo just as quickly as Willow had feared. She'd tried to remind herself that she couldn't focus all of her energy on how Maisie might get hurt if things didn't work out. She recalled her conversation with Roni: What if things *did* go well? What if Maisie and Theo had a perfectly lovely time together, and rather than being scarred for life by disappointment, Maisie simply formed some positive memories?

She had to admit that it was nice to have someone willing to help with Maisie, without having to impose on her neighbors. After their first visit to Theo's house, he'd begun dropping by Willow's place on weekends to check in on Maisie and to see if Willow wanted some time to herself. At first, Willow was hesitant to leave Maisie and Theo to their own devices, but Maisie was always thrilled to see Theo, especially when he began to bring Bixby on his visits. And there were certain days, especially after a long workweek, where it felt positively decadent to have time for a nap or some reading on weekend afternoons.

They'd had to set some ground rules at first. Theo had thought it might be fun to give Maisie some cooking lessons.

"Maybe start with something small, like pouring a bowl of cereal," Willow had suggested.

"Don't worry about it," said Theo. "We've

got this." Maisie had outfitted him in a number of Mardi Gras beads, and was herself wearing a long feather boa. She seemed to delight in dressing Theo in the most garish accessories she could find from her dressing-up box, and Theo submitted to this with good humor.

"Are you sure?" Willow said.

"It's fine. I've been teaching my nieces and nephews to bake since they were toddlers. I'll be doing most of the work, and Maisie will help."

"She does love to help," said Willow, bemused. She'd taken a lovely nap, and forty minutes later awoke to pancake batter on the kitchen ceiling.

"We made pamcakes!" Maisie announced, bursting with pride. Theo's expression was somewhat more shamefaced.

"Things…got a little out of hand," he said as Willow surveyed the wreckage. Cracked eggs on the linoleum floor, seven different mixing bowls in various stages of cleanliness and batter coating the stove, ceiling and cupboards.

"I would say so," she said, shaking with silent laughter. "It looks like you let Maisie help a lot."

"Oh, yes. Every step of the way, in fact."

"Well. As long as you had fun."

"We did," Maisie said, her eyes shining. "Try the pamcake, Mummy. I made it."

Theo's eyes were shining, too, and Willow could see how happy it made him to have made something with his daughter. Even if the kitchen now held more mess than it did pancakes.

But after he'd cleaned her kitchen, it smelled even nicer than before they'd started, so she didn't mind.

She was a little nervous, but mostly pleased, to see that he and Maisie were getting on so well together. As for Theo and herself...she never thought she'd regret their decision to proceed slowly. But as they continued to spend time together, she was finding it increasingly difficult to hold back. She wanted him. Her skin felt afire every time he touched her. If he put an arm around her or helped her with her coat, it was all she could do not to burst into flames. But the rational part of her was able to maintain a tenuous control, just enough so that she was able to keep herself from making any decisions she'd regret. She had responsibilities. She couldn't let physical desire override her judgment.

She threw herself into her work, hoping she could distract herself. Of course, Theo was at work, too, so it wasn't as if he wasn't on her mind there, as well. But then again, he wasn't around as much as he'd been at first. She supposed that made sense. He only did clinical work part-time, after all, and the rest of the time he did research. He'd begun setting up a number of research studies through St. Victoria Hospital so that patients who couldn't afford treatment could be part of research trials and have their care supported by grant funding. Setting up the research trials took up much of his time, he said, and so he was often away from the clinic and working late hours.

With Theo so busy, they didn't have much time to talk at work. He always seemed to be rushing off to St. Victoria Hospital for one appointment or another. But Willow didn't mind. She was glad that Theo was starting to fit in at his new job, and she was proud that he was doing research he was passionate about. She did miss seeing him as often as she'd used to, though. Just a few weeks ago, she'd never have thought she could miss seeing him at work. Yet here she was, thinking about his presence, his smile…his hands, steady and strong, pressing against her waist as they stole a moment together.

"Willow. Are you thinking about Theo again?" Roni's eyes twinkled from where she lay on her gurney, Buttons curled up beside her.

"Nonsense. I'd never let my personal life distract me at work," Willow said, lying through her teeth. She smiled and whispered, "Keep it down! We don't want anyone at work finding out just yet."

"But I need details! Have you two done the deed yet?"

Willow was about to protest, but then gave up, knowing that Roni was relentless in her pursuit of information. "We're taking it slow."

"Slow!" Roni scoffed. "Youth is wasted on the young."

"Besides, he's been very busy lately. He has to do a lot of running back and forth between here and St. Victoria Hospital. So we haven't been able to see each other much."

Roni frowned. "What could possibly be more important to this young man than spending time with you?"

"Oh, no, it's not like that! I just know that it's a lot of work to adjust to a new job, and Theo is still figuring out how to manage everything."

Roni still looked perturbed, and in an effort to change the subject, Willow said, "Your prognosis is still looking very good, despite what the press might say." The doom and gloom headlines about Roni's treatment persisted, with the press claiming that Roni was practically at death's door.

"I suppose telling everyone that I'm dying sells more papers than the truth."

"Still, you might want to think about having one of your assistants give them a little information. They could send out a press release, or at least give a quote about your condition."

At first, Roni and the clinic staff had agreed that as the press was so pushy, they shouldn't be given any information. Everyone had hoped that if the press realized there was no information to be had, they would simply go away. But the press encampment outside the clinic property had only got larger over the past few weeks, and the misinformation they were printing had become increasingly egregious.

"Hmm. I suppose they've stewed long enough. I'll hold a press conference. That way I can update them on my condition and announce the donation I'm making, as well. I think pledging a few million to support healthcare programs for the residents of St. Victoria should be enough to distract the press from their obsession with my health, and focus on that story instead."

"Roni, that's wonderful. The island will be

able to do some wonderful things with that kind of funding."

"Least I can do. St. Victoria is a special place. And while I do love coming here to beat cancer in style, I'll love it even more knowing that everyone has access to the help they need." Roni threw back her blankets and sat up. "Time to get back to work. Let's set this press conference up and give the sharks their feeding frenzy."

Theo turned his car up the long parkway toward the clinic's main entrance. Most days, he spent his mornings at St. Victoria Hospital, where he set up research studies, and then headed for the Island Clinic in the afternoon to work with patients. He found that he liked the variety of his work a great deal. He also didn't mind traveling the short distance between both medical centers every day. His schedule was flexible enough that the brief commute didn't add any pressure. But more importantly, he was able to attend his own medical appointments at St. Victoria Hospital as often as needed, without drawing anyone else's attention.

When he'd set up his medical care at St. Victoria Hospital, he'd done so with the express goal of not wanting to alert Willow that there was anything amiss. He'd worried that he would face questions from other doctors about his decision not to use the Island Clinic's resources, but apparently plenty of clinic staff got their care at St. Victoria Hospital, and vice versa, both as a professional courtesy and to minimize conflicts of interest. So the care team at St. Victoria Hospital hadn't been surprised that he was arranging for his care there at all. He'd had the biopsy done, and now had only to wait the typical four to six weeks for the results. His medical team had been reassuring that all signs continued to indicate that he was still in remission. The important thing was to keep his spirits up while they waited for the results.

He'd heard it all before. Cancer was all about measuring and waiting, and keeping morale high while one measured and waited. He tried not to think about it, but he did worry that Willow might have noticed that he was hiding something from her. He'd had to slip out of the clinic frequently over the past few weeks in order to establish care with new doctors, and then had to work late to make up for lost time. He'd told her that he was still adjusting to his new job, but he worried she might suspect it was more than that.

He still felt guilty about breaking his promise to Willow. But technically, he was within the letter of the law. He'd promised to keep her updated about any changes in his health, but really, a test wasn't a change. It was just a procedure to find out whether there *had been* a change. So there was no need to put Willow through the stress of waiting to get the biopsy results with him. If it turned out they were clear, he might not ever need to tell her about it at all.

The closer he became to Willow and Maisie, the more certain he was that he didn't want to tell Willow about the biopsy. The days he spent with Maisie were everything he'd hoped they would be. He delighted in spending time with his daughter, doing all the little things he'd imagined doing with a child of his own. They'd baked cookies together—with extremely careful supervision and somewhat less helping from Maisie, after the pancake fiasco—took long walks on the beach discovering interesting shells and pebbles and had dress-up tea parties. He was loving every minute of it.

But as he felt himself growing closer to both of them, he also wondered, again, if he could let himself have a family of his own. How could the three of them ever be a real family when the threat of cancer loomed over him? When he'd gone into remission, his doctors had reminded him to take things one day at a time. But it was hard not to focus on his worries and fears about the future when he was awaiting biopsy results. Did he have the right to ask Willow to join him for a lifetime of worrying that the cancer might come back someday? There was no way to know if he would have multiple cancer scares throughout his life, or if this most recent biopsy would be the last time he'd have to go through this. With such little certainty, could he allow himself to get close to Willow, knowing that there was a chance he'd have to rely on her for much greater support in the near future? He wasn't sure if that was fair to Willow, or to Maisie.

As he drove up the Island Clinic parkway, he saw Roni standing on the edge of the clinic grounds, with a few of the staff behind her. He could recognize Willow's petite frame, even from this distance, because she was a head or two shorter than the rest of the staff. She was surrounded by a phalanx of press, and she was holding a giant, oversize check. *Good, a press conference*, Theo thought. About time. The press was getting out of control with the amount of unsubstantiated rumors they were printing. And it looked as though Roni was announcing a donation, as well. Nate should be pleased. Theo also noticed that there was a heavy security presence. He was glad Nate had taken his caution about the overzealousness of the press seriously.

As he parked and stepped out of his car, he heard an uproar from the crowd. Roni's French bulldog had somehow broken away from her—Theo couldn't see clearly, but he thought it might have been lured away by one of the reporters—and was running across the lawn. One of the reporters lunged for the small dog. To his horror, he saw that Willow had chased the dog and was leaning forward to pick it up, out of the reporter's grasp. But the reporter, who was fairly large, had gathered too much momentum to stop running, and moments later, he was tackled by an even larger security guard.

Theo watched in horror as they all went down together—the reporter falling on top of Willow, who collapsed to the ground as the security guard fell on top of both of them. The dog had made its way safely back to Roni, but Theo barely had time to register this as he sprinted across the lawn. Both men were slowly getting to their feet as he arrived, but Willow wasn't moving. Under other circumstances, Theo, who had never been violent in his life, might have felt compelled to beat both the reporter and the security guard to a pulp, but at the moment, all his attention was focused on Willow.

After what felt like years, he finally reached her. Gently, he turned her over. He'd been alarmed that she was so still, but her eyes fluttered open. She motioned to her throat and made a strained noise, and he realized she'd had the wind knocked out of her. "Easy," he said. "You'll be all right in a few minutes. I'm going to take you inside so we can make sure you're okay."

He scooped Willow into his arms and headed toward the clinic. He couldn't believe the utter carelessness of the other two men, the blatant disregard they'd shown for Willow's well-being.

Once inside, he took Willow into an exam room and sat her down on the exam table. Her breathing was already easier; she was sitting upright on her own.

He began to feel her limbs, gently, to check for any other injuries, but she stopped him and shook her head. He cupped her cheek with his hand, stroking her hair, as they waited for her breath to recover.

Finally, she said, "I'm all right. Just winded."

Relief flooded through him, to be quickly replaced by anger. "*Just* winded? That reporter should be in jail. That security guard should be fired."

"It was an accident. No one was hurt."

"*You* were hurt." He resumed his examination, palpating her shoulders, her collarbone.

"Stop. Theo. It's all right. I'm fine." She reached up and turned his face toward hers. "I'm fine."

He found he was trembling. At first he'd thought he was shaking in anger, but now he realized that it was fear, as well. When he'd seen Willow lying on the grass, so still, he'd thought the worst. The idea of Willow being hurt, of losing Willow, was unbearable.

Without thinking, he pulled her close to him, her head against his chest. "I was so worried," he said. "I thought I'd lost you."

"Nonsense," she said, tilting her face up toward his. "I'm right here."

He gave her a light kiss, meant to reassure them both. He needed the comfort as much as she did. But his lips lingered, just before he pulled away, and then he didn't pull away at all. Their kiss deepened, her mouth yielding to his, her lips soft and pliable. His tongue began to explore her mouth, and he noticed that she tasted of honey, cinnamon and something else. Something that was indefinable yet tantalizing all the same.

She reached up from where she sat on the table to put her arms around his neck and pull him closer to her. He wanted to tell her that if they didn't stop now, he wasn't sure if he'd be able to, but then his nose was buried in the rich, dark hair that fell just so against the crook of her neck. His hands went to her waist, and then, gently, he traced the rise of one breast, just below the top of her blouse. *Go slow*, he reminded himself, *we agreed to go slow*.

But holding Willow in his arms stirred every feeling that had been reawakened since their first sunset kiss on the boardwalk. For weeks he'd been trying to pace himself, using every last bit of willpower to keep himself from asking for anything more than she was willing to offer. It didn't help matters much that he'd barely touched a woman during the four years before he'd met Willow—and now, restraint was nearly impossible as he drank in the warmth of her body, her hands raking through his hair.

There hadn't been a day that went by since his arrival on St. Victoria that he hadn't dreamed of holding her in his arms, just like this. To stop now would be agony, and yet…they'd agreed to go slow. Somehow, he managed to pull himself away from her just long enough to whisper, "Should we stop?"

Willow's eyes met his, her lips wet, her breathing heavy. In response, she shifted herself toward the edge of the table so that her body melted into his. He shivered, then groaned as he felt her press against him, and he began to feel himself grow hard. Now there was a new kind of agony as he became enveloped in the sensation of her: the smooth skin of her thighs beneath his hands, the sweet citrus scent of her hair and the heat of her lips on his. He was surrounded by the warmth of her, and yet still he burned with wanting her.

He had no thought, no awareness, beyond the softness of her skin against his hands, the smell of cinnamon enveloping them both and the warm curves of her body that seemed to meld into him. And so it came as surprise when he heard a knock on the exam room door.

"Hello?" called one of the nurses from the hallway outside.

They broke apart in a panic. Theo tucked his shirt back in and smoothed the wrinkles, while Willow did up the top buttons of her blouse.

"Theo? Willow?" It sounded like Talia's voice.

"Just a minute," Willow called back.

"We just wanted to check and make sure that Willow was all right," Talia called again.

"I'm fine," Willow replied. "Just a little winded. A little out of breath. Just give me a couple more minutes and I'll be right out."

There was a rather long pause, and then Talia said, "Okay. Just let me know if you need anything."

They were both silent until they heard the sound of Talia's receding footsteps, and then Willow erupted into laughter.

"I don't know how you can possibly laugh right now," Theo said. He couldn't believe what he'd just done. After all their talk of taking things slowly, he'd gone and acted like some sort of caveman, practically taking Willow right on the exam room table. What must she be thinking of him?

Seeing her knocked to the ground out on the lawn must have activated some sort of primal urge in him. And he'd been so relieved to see that she was all right that he'd got carried away with his feelings.

Fortunately, Willow didn't seem to mind. Far from it. "Do you think they know?" she said, jerking her head toward the door.

"Well, we've been trying to keep our relationship a secret, so I'm certain the whole clinic knows about it. As for whether they know about what we were doing just now… let's hope they trust in our professionalism."

Willow bit her lip. "Let's hope so indeed."

As she stood up to leave, straightening her skirt, Theo put his hand on hers. "Wait."

He was about to apologize. But then he remembered how much Willow valued honesty. And he would never, ever be sorry for the moment they'd just had.

"Do you think you can get a sitter for Maisie tonight?"

"Why? Do I have plans for tonight?"

"I very much hope you do."

Mrs. Jean was all too happy to watch Maisie for the evening.

"Don't even think about it," she said when Willow tried to apologize for the short notice. "It's about time you started getting serious about someone. Shall I assume it's that doctor I've seen coming over to your place all month?"

"His name's Theo. We've only been seeing each other a little bit, but…it's going very well."

"I would hope so. He's over here often enough. Why don't you pack an overnight bag for Maisie, so you can pick her up in the morning? That way you don't have to worry about rushing home early tonight."

"Oh, that's not necessary. I'm sure I'll be home by eleven."

"Sweetheart. Pack Maisie a bag. And maybe one for yourself, too. If you come back tonight, fine. But if you do end up spending the night with this young gentleman, then at least you won't need to worry about rushing home." Willow nodded in agreement, and the older woman cackled. "That's what I thought. Tonight's the night."

Willow was so flushed with excitement that she couldn't even fend off Mrs. Jean's insinuations. Besides, Mrs. Jean was right, if that moment with Theo in the exam room was any indication of his intentions. Tonight *was* the night.

For the first time in years, tonight was the night.

As she packed her things—a toothbrush, a change of clothes for work tomorrow—she could barely keep her hands from shaking. That exam room kiss had turned into something more so rapidly that she hadn't had time to think. But then Theo had suggested that she come over tonight so that they could do things properly, without the worry of unlocked doors and the hundreds of other things that could go wrong with intimacy in a workplace setting.

She'd immediately agreed, but then she'd spent the rest of the day thinking about it. And worrying about it.

She was so out of practice. What if Theo noticed?

In the exam room, she hadn't had time to think. It had happened so suddenly that instinct had just taken over. But now she'd spent an entire day thinking about what awaited her in the evening. Her skin burned with a heat she hadn't felt in ages. She'd almost forgotten what it felt like to want someone so badly that it seemed almost impossible to get close enough to them. In fact, she wasn't certain if she'd ever wanted anyone the way she wanted Theo.

She hoped she wouldn't embarrass herself. But she also knew that it didn't matter. Nothing, not even potential embarrassment, was going to stop her from feeling Theo's hands on her skin again. She could still feel the warmth where he'd cupped her cheek.

She decided to drive the short distance to Theo's house, just in case she did end up spending the night.

Once again, he and Bixby were waiting on the porch.

She got out of her car, hoping he couldn't see her knees knocking. Why was she so nervous? It was Theo, she thought. He'd become so familiar to her over these past few weeks. Most of the time, his presence was warm and comforting.

Perhaps, she thought, she was nervous because she didn't want warmth just now.

She wanted flames.

She somehow made herself walk up the porch steps. He slipped an arm around her waist and held her close, and she let herself lean into his arms. Nervous as she was, she was grateful for the support. Then a flicker of light inside the house caught her eye, and she looked over his shoulder, through the doorway.

"Oh, Theo," she breathed. "It's beautiful."

The lights inside the house were dim, and dozens of small candles dotted the front entryway and living room. White and red rose petals were scattered everywhere, including a trail to the bedroom.

He leaned in close and murmured into her hair. "Four years."

"What?"

"That's how long it's been for me. Longer, in fact, although I never kept an exact count. I haven't been with anyone for four years. And you said that it had been a long time for you, too. So I thought, since it's the first time in a long time for both of us, that I should do something to make it special."

She raised a hand to his cheek, feeling the faint stubble there. "Tonight's already special."

He kissed her, a gentle, searching kiss that quickly deepened. She felt the warmth that had kindled deep within her begin to spread, and as he traced her arm with one finger, she shivered.

"Are you cold?" he said.

"Not exactly."

He smiled. "Maybe we should go inside all the same."

He led her up the rose petal path to the bedroom. There were only a few candles there, casting dim shadows on the walls.

It was very romantic. But it was also very dark. And Willow thought she might know why.

"Theo," she said, "are you nervous about me seeing you?"

He let out a long breath, and she realized he must have been even more nervous than she was.

"I should have known you would guess," he said.

"Tell me." She waited in the darkness.

"I've lost a lot of weight from the cancer. My body's changed. I don't look like me anymore. At least, not how I remember myself. No one's really seen me since before I started treatment. This is my first time doing *this* the way I look now, and I'm not sure what it will be like."

She kissed the corner of his mouth, right where it always seemed about to pull up into a smile. "I know you've been through some changes. And that we're both scared. But let's not hide from each other tonight."

The candlelight flickered, catching at the gold flecks in his hazel eyes. "What could you possibly have to hide from me?"

She swallowed. "That it's been such a long time since I've done this that I might…lose control. And that I'm afraid of what you might think, if you see me like that."

Now his eyes were ablaze, and she didn't think it was just from candlelight. "I think I might like to see you lose control."

"I think you almost did, earlier this morning."

"Mmm. And it was almost every bit as lovely as I might have hoped."

"Almost?"

"Well, we were constrained by our circumstances. And caught up in the moment. I didn't, for example, have the opportunity to do this." He leaned her against the back of the bedroom wall and kissed the hollow of her throat. She tilted her chin upward to give him greater access, her skin humming against her.

"Or this," he said as his hands went to the back of her neck to undo the clasp of her halter dress. Once undone, the top fell to her waist, her breasts exposed. He cupped one of them, his fingers caressing, then gently pulling and teasing one nipple. She arched her back, moaning, to press herself more firmly into his palm.

He knelt before her, kissing between her breasts, her stomach, as he made his way downward. "Or, of course, this," he whispered, pulling her dress from her hips. There was a soft crumple as it hit the floor. He gazed up at her, his chin level with the tops of her thighs, and slowly slid her panties from her hips.

She could feel his soft breath against the tuft of hair between her legs, and then, almost before she knew what was happening, he'd buried his face in the warmth there, and she felt the slow strokes of his tongue. She tried to tell him that he didn't have to, that no one had *ever*, but somehow her words were lost, and all that came out were gasps of air. Her knees were shaking; she didn't know how she could keep standing upright, but then she felt his hands on her thighs, holding her in place as he continued on with what he'd started. She began to see starbursts in front of her eyes, dark as the room was, and she moaned his name and told him she couldn't hold back.

He lifted her to the bed then, and she heard him racing to remove his clothes. There was the sound of a foil wrapper; she knew she could trust Theo to have planned on protection.

And not a moment too soon. Her body ached with a primal need; her skin was aflame, and she felt the yearning that had begun deep within her threaten to overwhelm her entirely. She could feel his body next to her on the bed. "Now," she breathed, and a moment later he had fully embedded himself in her. Her hips rocked upward to meet his, and he pushed himself into her, again and again, their bodies joining in a dance as old as time itself.

With each thrust, she felt herself getting closer to the point of no return, to the loss of control that she feared, and yet desperately craved. She felt his pace quicken, felt herself pushed to the brink, and then suddenly she cried his name again and let herself go. Her consciousness shattered into a thousand pieces, and for a moment there was nothing beyond his breath and hers, the sensation of their bodies moving together. And then, at last, there was the feeling of lying together, replete and exhausted, their limbs tangled together, their bodies apart.

How strange, she thought dreamily as her eyes began to close. A moment ago, she'd felt shattered into pieces. But now, somehow, she felt…whole.

CHAPTER EIGHT

THEO WOKE THE next morning to see Willow
fast asleep on the pillow beside him. He slipped
out of bed quietly, so as not to wake her. She
worked so hard. She deserved her sleep.

Especially after the night before. What a
way to break a four-year dry spell. He smiled,
remembering how nervous they'd both been
at the start. Clearly, neither of them had had
anything to worry about. Or at least, Willow
hadn't. Theo was certain he'd never felt the
things he'd felt with Willow with anyone else
before. He hoped the night had been all she'd
wanted it to be. And if it hadn't, he hoped they
could practice until they got it right.

He headed toward the kitchen, wondering
what Willow might like for breakfast. As he
was pulling a loaf of bread from the refrigerator, his phone rang.

It was Becca. He listened to her chatter away
about family concerns. She mentioned that his

father had had a yearly checkup, and his Alzheimer's appeared to have plateaued, which was very good news. After a while, though, Becca noticed that he wasn't saying much.

"What's going on?" she said. "Why are you being so quiet?"

"I'm not," he said, trying to keep his voice low so that he wouldn't wake Willow in the other room. "I'm just listening to you."

"No, you're hardly saying anything. And now you're *speaking* quietly."

He was about to protest, but at that moment, Willow came tiptoeing down the hall, already dressed.

Sister, he mouthed quietly, pointing at the phone. Willow nodded and headed toward the door.

Damn. He didn't want to tell Becca about Willow, because doing so would undoubtedly result in shrieks of sisterly joy that he didn't want his ears subjected to this early in the morning. On the other hand, he didn't want Willow to leave without having breakfast. Or at least without saying goodbye.

"Hold on," he said into the phone. "Just give me one minute."

He caught Willow just as she was about to walk out the door.

"I was hoping you'd stay for breakfast."

"I can't. I have an early shift today. I should have been up an hour ago. I don't even have time for toast."

"You should have told me! I would have set the alarm earlier this morning."

"No, I needed the rest after last night. It's all right. I'll pick up a chocolate croissant when I get in."

"When can I see you again?"

"In about thirty minutes. I'm going to work, remember?"

"No, I mean when can I *see* you again?"

She gave him a quick kiss, just at the corner of his mouth. "As soon as possible."

He watched her leave, and then turned his attention back to his phone, where he could hear Becca's voice screeching.

"Who was that? They sounded female. What was a woman doing at your place this early in the morning?"

He sighed. Becca would find out eventually. And now that he had some coffee going, he thought he might be able to handle her reaction.

"That was Willow. She was just leaving."

"But isn't it, like, seven in the morning in the Caribbean? Why was she over just now?"

"She, ah…spent the night."

He had to hold the phone an arm's length

away from his ear as Becca gave an excited shriek.

"So what's the story with you two? Are you an item? When will the family meet her?"

"Not for a long time. We're taking it slow and seeing how it goes."

"You can't be taking it *that* slow. You've been there, what, a month and a half, and she's already sleeping over? When did this start?"

"Look, I'd be happy to fill you in on the details, but for right now, I don't want you to get overexcited, okay? This is a very new situation for both of us, and it's complicated, because it could affect Maisie. We don't want to add any more pressure than there already is."

"Okay. Got it. No pressure. But can I at least be happy for you?"

He couldn't help smiling. "I'm happy for me, so I guess it's okay if you are, too."

"You deserve it, little brother."

"Becca. We're twins."

"Yes, but I'm the five-minutes-older twin. Which makes me five minutes wiser, too. You've had plenty of tough stuff in your life. I'm glad you get some brightness, too."

He knew she meant well. But his sister could be very…effusive at times.

"Speaking of the tough stuff," she continued. "Did you get those biopsy results yet?"

"Still waiting. It usually takes four to six weeks, so I should get them any day now."

"How's Willow handling it? I'm sure she must be nervous."

"Um. Actually, I haven't told her about it."

"What? How could you not tell her?"

"The test results might be clear. I didn't see any reason to worry her unnecessarily."

"I don't believe it. This is so you. You're doing exactly what you always do."

"Which is what?"

"You're pushing people away, especially the people who could help you the most. You're distancing and cutting yourself off from people under the guise of protecting them."

"Well, that's just completely not true."

"I've seen you do it before. With the family. With Mum and Dad especially. Downplaying your cancer, being secretive about how your treatments were working out. Pretending that you weren't that tired or that the side effects weren't that bad. The way you were acting, anyone might have thought you had a touch of flu, rather than a life-threatening illness."

"That was different. Dad had just been diagnosed with Alzheimer's and Mum needed our help. She didn't need to worry about what was happening with me, too."

"I hate to say this, but what if things hadn't

gone well? What if Mum had learned that you'd died suddenly, and she didn't have any time to prepare for it?"

Theo shifted uneasily. "I never lied to her about anything."

"Sure, but you never volunteered information, either. You made it sound like cancer was a matter of a few chemo treatments and then you were done, rather than a four-year struggle for your life. We didn't even get to celebrate that you were in remission, because more than half the family didn't realize you'd had cancer in the first place."

"Which was as I wanted it. Being in remission was enough good news. Yes, it would have been nice to have everyone celebrate with me, but making sure no one knew the full extent of it was more important."

"Yes, but what you don't realize, Theo, is that I was the one everyone went to when they were trying to figure out how serious your cancer was. And I couldn't tell them anything, because I knew you'd never forgive me for it. It was so stupid, because everyone just wanted to help you. You could have had so much more support if you'd only let people in."

"Now hold on. That's exactly why I tried to keep everyone from finding out the full extent of what I was dealing with. You know how our family is. Everyone wants to know everything. Gossip flies fast, and if people get even the tiniest shred of news, suddenly our third cousin in Ibiza knows about it. I didn't want anything to get out, not just for my own desire for privacy, but because I also didn't want one of the aunts or cousins to call Mum and start telling her all about how I was struggling with the side effects."

"Look, I get why you did it, even if I don't necessarily agree with it. But if you keep shutting people out like this, eventually someone's going to get hurt. I know you do it because you want to protect everyone, but it comes off as though you don't want people involved in your life."

"It doesn't matter," he told her. "You don't know what it's like to have a serious illness. It's hard enough to deal with cancer without having to know about how much other people are worrying."

"Are you serious?" her voice cried from the phone. "I don't know what it's *like*?"

He instantly regretted his choice of words. Becca was the only person in his family that he'd confided in during the worst of the cancer, and he'd just been completely dismissive of her support. "I didn't mean that the way it sounded," he said, not quickly enough.

"I hope not." He'd never heard her sound so angry. "Because I was the one who was there on those nights that you supposedly didn't need to worry anybody. I was the one keeping your meds organized and driving you to the hospital when your fevers got too high."

"And I feel terrible that you were in that position."

"I wanted to be in that position! I'm your sister, Theo. Even if you don't want me, I'm going to be there for you. That's what family does—they stick by each other when things are tough. Not just for the good times, but for the difficult bits, too. And I'm certain that Willow will want to be there for you through this."

"I'll think about it," he said, because he knew Becca wouldn't let this go unless he at least pretended to acknowledge changing his mind. In any other situation, he might have agreed with her. But she just didn't understand how he felt. She couldn't, unless she'd been in the same situation herself. He hoped she never would be.

"You do that. Think about it a lot," Becca said. "And… I'll be thinking about you, and hoping your biopsy comes through clear. Because I care about you. In fact, you've got a lot of people who care about you. So don't shut us out, okay?"

They ended their call and Theo went onto the porch to have his toast and coffee next to Bixby. The dog settled his head on Theo's knee, and Theo scratched just the right spot behind his ears.

He felt guilty about what he'd said to Becca, and even guiltier that she'd shouldered so much of the burden of worrying about his health. It had been so hard for him to open up to her that he'd never stopped to consider that she might have appreciated being able to share her worries about him with someone else. But of course, she'd kept his secrets and respected his privacy as best she could, because she was his sister. He felt a wave of affection for her, even though he still didn't think she understood why he had to keep his biopsy a secret from Willow.

When Theo went to go back inside, the dog placed his paw on the door and looked at him with his usual pleading eyes. "No, Bixby," Theo said firmly. "You know you live out here." The dog whined, and Theo rubbed his sides to reassure him. "Come on, you've got a perfectly nice bed and all your toys on the porch."

There was nothing he would have liked more than to bring the dog inside. He'd had a dog as a child, and he'd always wanted one as an adult, but he'd been so busy in medical school that he'd never had the time. And then the cancer had hit soon after, and he could barely take care of himself, let alone a dog.

And now, just when he was trying to prove that he could take care of his own child, he was also facing the worry that his cancer might come back. He couldn't stomach his anger toward the cancer. It ruined everything in his life. The cancer had been the reason he'd stayed away from his daughter in the first place, hoping he could protect her from grief. When he'd entered remission, he'd decided that he couldn't live his life as though the threat of a recurrence of cancer was always in the background. He was tired of letting cancer control his decisions, tired of letting it take away everything he wanted.

He'd missed the first three years of his daughter's life because of cancer. Or because of his desire to protect her from the emotional impact of his cancer. At the time, he'd been so certain he was making the right decision. But over the past few weeks, he'd been faced with the full realization of everything he'd missed. Maisie's deep, full-body chuckle; her preoccupation with the little rocks and shells she found on the beach; the warmth of her hand in his. Now that he knew her, his heart ached at how much he'd missed. For weeks, he'd been wrestling with the decision he'd made more than three years ago. He'd tried to tell himself that there was no use dwelling on it; he couldn't change the past. But he knew now that if he were faced with the same decision today, he could not have made the same choice. It had been hard enough to stay out of Maisie's life without having ever met her. Now that he knew his daughter, he'd never be able to leave her again.

The thought scared him. Because as much as he blamed the cancer for some of the losses in his life, the cancer wasn't the only thing that had held him back. He'd chosen not to meet Maisie. Just as he'd chosen to cut himself off from his family's support. He'd told himself that he was doing what was best for them, but…was he really? Becca's words had had more of an impact than he'd realized at first. What if his mum had learned he'd died suddenly, without any chance to prepare?

And what if something had happened to Willow, while she'd been caring for Maisie by herself for the past three years? Maisie would have been completely on her own. He recalled that Willow had mentioned her gran had set up a trust for Maisie, but it sounded as though it wasn't much. He felt sick at the thought of Maisie being left so alone. His own daughter, a child with an extensive number of relatives who would happily cherish her, would have been orphaned. Had he really protected her at all by staying away?

Bixby brushed against his legs. The dog had an unabashed love for him. Banishing him to the porch hadn't diminished his attachment to Theo at all. In fact, the only effect it had had was that Theo often found himself rather sad that he couldn't have the dog with him more often. He remembered when Willow had told him that keeping the dog on the porch was a sign that he was scared. Well, that was true enough. He was scared for his health, and he was scared of letting down everyone he cared about.

But if he was too afraid to let a dog into his home, how could he ever allow himself to get close to Willow? Or to his own daughter? He was so afraid of letting them down that he wasn't doing a good job of being there for them in the first place. He was breaking a promise to Willow, right now, by not telling her that he was awaiting biopsy results, and he might tell himself that it was to protect her, but the truth was that he was afraid of making his worst fears real. But keeping the biopsy a secret didn't place him in any less danger, or put him at any less risk of letting Willow and Maisie down.

He had to tell Willow about the biopsy. He just hoped she would understand why he'd kept it a secret for so long.

It had been a long time since Willow had felt this good in the morning.

Oh, she enjoyed most mornings, but *this* one was special. She sipped her coffee as she finished her chart reviews in one of the nurses' offices. Everyone seemed especially friendly as she'd come in to work, and she had a feeling that they might be responding to something they saw in her. There was a kind of lightness that she felt within herself. The day was like any other, and yet it seemed to be full of possibility.

She didn't have to think too hard about what was different. Last night with Theo had been positively decadent. She might not have dated much in her past, but she was certain that she'd never felt the things she'd felt last night with anyone. Theo had been so… She shivered, thinking about it.

If it had been hard to concentrate at work before, then it was going to be nearly impossible now. She would have to find some way to keep her mind off him.

And so she tried to focus on the other things that brought her joy. It seemed as though everything she loved in her life had been turned up in volume, as if her night with Theo had left her with a heightened sensitivity to all that was good in life. Mrs. Jean had texted her a picture of a still-sleeping Maisie that morning, and Willow reveled as always in the chubby hands and full cheeks. Someone had already started the coffee when she got to work, and it was made to perfection. She'd managed to snag a chocolate croissant before they were all gone, and she thought it might be the best bit of pastry she'd ever had in her life. The entire world felt as though it were tinted with a soft, warm glow.

She was thoroughly enjoying her morning, and was just about to wrap up her chart review and begin seeing patients, when the phone rang in the nurse's office.

She picked up; it was a lab technician from St. Victoria Hospital.

They had faxed over some lab work for a patient, and wanted to make sure it had come through. Willow thought that was a little unusual, since the clinic had its own lab and was unlikely to use the hospital's. She found the results on the fax machine and let the technician know they'd arrived.

Normally, she checked the name of the ordering physician on the lab charts and put them in the corresponding file folders. But this time, something caught her eye. The lab tech had mistakenly typed Theo's name in the "patient" section.

It was probably a mistake. Although the staff at St. Victoria Hospital rarely made mistakes. Still, it was an easy enough oversight.

She dropped the lab work into Theo's file. She couldn't help noticing, at a glance, that the paperwork included biopsy results.

A distant alarm began to ring in her mind. She did her best to ignore it. But the thought kept returning to her mind: What if it wasn't a mistake? What if Theo had indeed been the patient?

If he had been, then it was none of her business. She should respect his confidentiality, as she would in any other professional situation.

Except Theo had promised to keep her updated of any changes regarding his remission status. And that fax had contained biopsy results. With Theo's name listed as the patient.

But Theo couldn't have had a biopsy. That was exactly the kind of thing he'd promised he would tell her about.

Unless Theo didn't keep his promises.

Unable to restrain herself any longer, she

dove back into Theo's file and retrieved the test results. They were the results of a biopsy that had been done a few weeks ago, confirming that a skin lesion on the patient's arm was benign. The patient was clearly listed as Theo Moore.

The biopsy was clear. That fact rang within her head. She wanted to be relieved. *Was* relieved. Except her heart was breaking. Why wouldn't Theo tell her he was waiting on biopsy results after he'd promised to keep her abreast of any changes regarding his health? Didn't he think she cared about him? Didn't he want her to be there for him, no matter what he was facing?

And worst of all, if that was how he felt—if he didn't want her to be there for him—then why had he promised to keep her informed?

He'd just been telling her what he thought she wanted to hear. Just like Jamie. Rather than the truth, he'd said what sounded good in the moment.

She heard footsteps at the doorway and looked up to see Theo standing there.

"Those are my test results," he said.

"I know. Your biopsy was clear." She needed to tell him right away. She could deal with the tears that she was struggling to hold back in just a moment. But Theo must have been agonizing over these results for weeks—all the while, of course, not telling her that he was worried—and he should learn the results as soon as he could.

"Well, that's a relief."

"Yes, I'm sure it is." The anger was coming into her voice now, despite her attempts to hold it back. "When were you going to tell me that you had a biopsy done?"

"Just now," he said. "I came here to tell you about it."

"Oh, well, that's very convenient. Because the results were faxed over from St. Victoria a few seconds ago. So that's interesting that you were just about to tell me, just now."

Her head felt very strange, and she realized a headache was beginning. The kind that started when she was trying not to cry.

"Congratulations," she said, trying muster her emotions. "You're healthy." She was trying so hard to feel the relief she should feel. This was good news. She should be happy. They both should be. Except why hadn't Theo told her about it in the first place? Why had she found out about this by accident? Had he *ever* been planning to tell her about it?

"Oh," he said, his smile small and forced. "That's good news, isn't it?"

The tears welled in her eyes, and she blinked

furiously to hold them back. "How long have you been waiting for these results?"

"A little over a month."

"A little..." She couldn't finish; she was too overwhelmed by disbelief. "And you never thought to tell me about it?"

"I hoped I wouldn't have to. I know you're a worrier. And I didn't want you to have to worry about this."

"This is why you've been running back and forth between the clinic and the hospital so much, isn't it? You told me that you were just adjusting to your new job and your new schedule. But it's also because you're probably getting your medical care there. It makes sense. You've only just gone into remission. It stands to reason you'd have to attend plenty of follow-up appointments. But what does not make sense, Theo, is why you would ever try to hide that from me. Why you wouldn't just be open about where you were going and what you were doing."

"Because I wanted to spare you from all that! It's bad enough that I have to deal with all the stress of it. I didn't want to put that on your shoulders, too. Especially because I hoped that the biopsy would be clear. I thought, what was the point of worrying you if it would all turn out to be nothing?"

"The point, Theo, is that you promised me that you'd let me know of any changes with your health."

"But does it matter, now that we know the results are clear? Nothing's changed. I was in remission a few weeks ago, and I'm in remission now."

"Yes—after weeks of worrying about the biopsy, without ever giving me a hint of what you were going through. I'm glad you're healthy, Theo, but I'm very, very concerned you didn't tell me. I could have been there for you, instead of you having to wait for these results alone. Didn't you *want* me to be there for you?"

Asking the question almost broke her heart. She'd thought she meant something to Theo. But if he couldn't be transparent with her about something like this, then maybe she wasn't important to him at all.

He rushed forward and grabbed both of her hands. "I wanted to protect you."

"By shutting me out? That doesn't make me feel protected, Theo. It makes me feel like I don't matter."

"That's not true," he said. "There is *nothing* that matters to me more than you."

"Really?" she said. "Is this how you treat the people who matter to you? By being secretive? Withholding crucial information? That's not how you deal with a relationship, Theo—if this even is a relationship."

"I just wanted to spare you any stress. I had to hide everything, because I didn't want you to be upset."

She'd heard it before. It was Jamie all over again. Theo wasn't telling her the whole story because he didn't want to hurt her, when she was hurt far more by not knowing the truth. All this time, she'd thought they were growing closer, when in fact he hadn't even been able to tell her that he was waiting to hear whether he'd have to suffer the return of a life-threatening illness. How could he have kept such an enormous secret from her? Worse, how could he have acted for weeks as though nothing was bothering him? That was what upset her the most. She didn't want to be in a relationship with someone who kept her at arm's length and put up a facade.

Her dream of a family had always involved having a group of people who supported each other through tough times. But if Theo had thought it best to go through this alone—to put up a front, and shut her out from everything he was really feeling—then being with him put her further away from that goal than ever. It was that simple: if he couldn't be open with her, then he wasn't the right person for her.

Tears fell from her eyes despite her attempts to blink them back. This was exactly why she had sworn off relationships in the first place. She'd wasted so much of her life waiting for Jamie to be ready. She'd waited for an engagement, for marriage and for the family she'd believed they both wanted. But she couldn't wait any more. She had a life to live, and a daughter to take care of. Theo was never supposed to have been part of any of it. He'd simply arrived, without warning, and stirred feelings that she'd thought were long dormant. She was furious with him, but she was even more furious with herself for not realizing straight-away that those feelings would only lead to heartbreak.

"I think I understand," she said. "When you made that promise, you were telling me what you thought I wanted to hear."

"What I thought would be the least painful."

She shook her head. "I can't believe you're still trying to justify it."

He tried to put a hand on her shoulder, and she twisted away. "No," she said. "You promised you wouldn't do this. You know how important honesty is to me. I thought it was important to you, too. But instead, you hid things and kept secrets. You let me know only the information you thought would make me feel better, rather than the whole truth."

"I'm sorry," he said, and she could see that he meant it. He was beginning to blink back tears, too. "I'd do anything to change this. Anything to go back to a month from now and make a different decision. If I could do it over again, I'd tell you about the biopsy, I swear. My God, Willow, there's so much in my life I'd do differently if I had the chance."

She wished she could believe him. But over and over again, he'd shown her who he was.

"I don't know if that's true, Theo. Isn't this kind of what you do?"

He looked as though she'd slapped him.

"Think about it. You stayed away from Maisie, missed the first three years of your daughter's life, because you wanted to protect her from grief. You kept the extent of your cancer a secret from your family because you didn't want them to feel sad. You can't even let a dog into your house because you're worried about it getting attached to you. If you can't do that, then how do you expect to let a child into your life? You can't be a parent unless you're willing to put your whole heart into it. But your heart, Theo, is a secret. You *claim* to be protecting the people you care about, when all you're actually doing is hiding the truth from everyone, and keeping yourself emotionally cut off!"

She was shaking with emotion. Theo's face looked absolutely heartbroken, and it broke her heart to think that she was hurting him. But he'd hurt her first. And if he could hurt her that way, then she couldn't see any future with him. No matter how painful it might be to see her dreams fade away, she had to let them go. Because she couldn't be with someone who wasn't transparent with her.

"It's time to ask yourself who you're really protecting," she continued. "Because I sure as hell don't feel protected. I just feel lied to. Maybe this has nothing to do with protecting other people, and everything to do with protecting yourself."

"From what?" he whispered.

"I don't know. Maybe from getting close. Maybe from getting some of the things you want, only to have to be afraid of losing them again. But those are questions for you to ask yourself, Theo. I can't get hurt again while I'm waiting for you to figure them out."

"What are you saying?"

"I'm saying that this isn't working. It can't work. We're not..." She swallowed, trying to force the words out. "We're not right for each other. We'd just keep going around in circles.

You'd keep hiding things from me, and I'd keep feeling betrayed."

"And what about Maisie?"

"This is exactly what I didn't want for her. I didn't want her getting attached, and then getting hurt."

"I never wanted that, either. But does it have to be that way?"

"I'm sorry, but it does. I think it's for the best if we don't tell her you're her father." The look on his face was absolutely devastating. It tore her heart into pieces to think that she was hurting him this much.

But she did not want her daughter to have an emotionally distant father. She had to protect her child.

"Please," he said. "Don't do this. I can change. I'll do anything to prove it to you."

She couldn't stop the tears that streamed down her cheeks. "It's too late."

Willow knew that one of the most important parts of getting through work in any medical setting was finding a good place to cry. Even when one wasn't going through personal heartbreak, her profession offered plenty of opportunities for tears. Losing a patient, an altercation with a colleague or just the simple stress of balancing home with work necessitated a thorough knowledge of all the quiet, private spaces that might be available if one ever needed a good cry.

Most of the nurses at the clinic shared their space, so she didn't have an office of her own. But she knew of a quiet nook in the clinic's courtyard that would afford some privacy. She often went there when she needed a quiet moment. The nook held a simple concrete bench, and was shielded by walls on two sides and by the tall flowers of a butterfly garden on the other. She went there now, hoping for some peace, and hoping to simply let her tears fall without having to worry about holding them back.

She had trusted Theo. Even in the face of all the signs not to, she had believed him when he'd said he would be honest with her. She'd felt that he deserved a second chance, after all he'd been through. And then she'd developed feelings for him, allowing herself to hope that maybe, just this once, growing close to someone wouldn't lead to heartbreak.

But here she was, in the same situation all over again. Only this time, it was worse, because Maisie was involved.

Maisie was clearly very attached to Theo. She loved visiting his house, loved playing with Bixby. And she loved playing games with

Theo. This was exactly the situation Willow had wanted to avoid: Maisie getting attached to someone who would then leave her life.

But was keeping Theo from Maisie the best option? A moment ago, she had been certain. By keeping his biopsy a secret, and acting as though everything was normal for several weeks—she shook her head, still unable to believe it—Theo had shown her that he couldn't be emotionally available. But she thought about Theo's extended family. If she didn't tell Maisie that Theo was her father, would she essentially be denying her daughter the chance to be someone's cousin, someone's niece? Someone's granddaughter? Willow's own gran couldn't be here for Maisie, but she still had a chance to have a grandmother. Reluctantly, she wondered if she might rethink her decision regarding Maisie's relationship with Theo. She didn't want her daughter to have an emotionally distant father, but nor did she want to keep her child from the opportunity to have close family relationships. She'd have to figure out what that would look like later. For now, she was still reeling from Theo's decision to lie to her.

He'd treated her just as Jamie had. He'd told her the things he thought she wanted to hear, rather than the truth. And then he'd tried to justify it by explaining that he'd held his silence because *she* would have been upset, a justification that only made everything much worse. As though she'd ever be upset by knowing the truth. Lies had caused her much greater pain than the truth ever could.

What was *wrong* with her? Was she simply drawn to manipulative men?

As much as she hated what Theo had done, it wasn't the worst part. The worst part was that she was so relieved that his biopsy had been clear. She wanted to celebrate that with him. But she couldn't. Theo had taken that chance for joy away from her because he'd shut her out.

She rubbed her temples, her head aching, as she again thought of what he'd said about protecting her. It made her so sad, to think of Theo carrying that lonely burden all by himself. He must have been so scared while he was waiting for the test results. It scared her, too, to think of losing him. But how much scarier to go through that alone. If she and Theo stayed together, she might not be able to trust him to keep her informed about everything. What if she lost him unexpectedly, without time to prepare, because he'd withheld important information in a misguided attempt to "protect" her? Some people might prefer it that way, but it wasn't what Willow wanted. She thought she'd been clear about that. She *had* been clear about that. Theo just hadn't listened.

As much as she feared the thought of losing Theo, the thought of being kept in the dark was even more frightening. She was a critical care nurse. She knew that there were many things in life that were scary. She didn't want to hide from them; she wanted to find someone she could trust, so they could be together through all the scary things. It broke her heart that that person wasn't Theo.

CHAPTER NINE

THEO DIDN'T KNOW how he was able to get himself to work over the next few days, but he managed somehow. He might have felt as though his heart had been ripped from his chest were it not for the occasional pangs that shot through it, letting him know that his heart was indeed still there, still beating and still broken.

He hadn't seen Willow for several days. He knew nothing of the details of her absence, only that she'd taken a few days off. He hoped that she wasn't alone, in pain, because of him. When he'd first gotten to know Willow, he'd been struck by how independent she was, and also how alone. He, at least, had Becca to talk to, and if he'd wanted to, he had more family anytime he needed them. Who did Willow talk to about her heartbreak? Was she feeling heartbreak? He didn't know what would feel worse, the thought of her getting over their relationship quickly, or the thought of her grieving by herself, with no one to give her comfort or support.

He should be that person, giving her support. Instead, he was the person who'd caused her pain. Something he promised himself he'd never do. But then, it seemed he was in the habit of breaking promises these days. Even to himself.

Even though it was hard to focus at work, he was grateful for the distraction that his patients and his research provided. Shifting his attention to his clinical work helped to ease his heartbreak a bit, although of course it was always there, waiting, when he was finished for the day.

He found himself lingering at the clinic after his shifts were over, reluctant to go home with just Bixby for company and face the emptiness there. He spent extra time checking in with his patients, who seemed grateful for his concern, albeit a little surprised by the late hours he was keeping.

One patient was especially blunt.

"Shouldn't you be home by now?" asked Roni. Theo had been taking his time in wrapping up his rounds for the day, and had checked in on Roni more than once.

"I'm staying late tonight to get through some

paperwork and thought I'd check in," he responded. "Didn't mean to bother you."

"It's no bother. I just thought that all doctors hit the golf course after four p.m. Glad to be proven wrong."

"I hear you'll be leaving us soon," he said. Roni had her final dose of chemotherapy scheduled within the week, and all signs indicated that her tumor was shrinking. "You'll need to be closely monitored to make sure things continue to go well. But if the cancer cells continue to recede for at least a month, we'll be able to officially say that you're in remission."

"Well, that's good news. I won't miss being sick, but I will miss this place."

"Are you sure you don't want to stay here, where we can keep an eye on you?"

She sighed. "As nice as that sounds, it's time for me to get back to the real world. This has been a very nice pretend vacation. And I do think pretending to be on vacation was just what I needed to get through chemo. But I'm ready to get back to my life, and my work. What about you, Doc? Are you ready to face reality yet?"

"What do you mean?"

"No offense, Doc, but your expression says a little more than 'I'm bummed to be at work late.' You look positively mopey. If I didn't know better, I might wonder if you're here late because you're hiding from something."

He forced a smile. "It's nothing."

"Nothing you want to talk about with me, anyway. That's fine. You know who's a good person to talk things over with? My favorite nurse. Who I'm pretty sure was *your* favorite nurse, up until a few days ago."

He winced. "How much do you know?"

"She hasn't told me anything. But I know a lovers' quarrel when I see one. Did you do something stupid?"

"Yes, I think maybe I did."

She sighed. "That's very unfortunate. I haven't seen her for a few days, and I miss having her around."

"Me, too."

"What happened?"

"I really screwed up," he said, and then found he simply couldn't continue. His voice caught in his throat. He'd made the same mistake so many times. He'd done it with Maisie, keeping himself out of her life so that she wouldn't be hurt by the loss of a parent. He'd meant to protect her, but instead he simply hadn't been there for her. And then with Willow, by doing the same thing that her ex had done to her. And now he might have lost Willow forever.

It can't be too late, he thought. *It just can't be.*

Roni was waiting patiently. He didn't feel pressured to speak, but he had the distinct impression that she was willing to listen, if he wanted to talk.

"I promised I'd always be open with her," he said. "And then I wasn't. I kept a secret, to protect her."

"Sounds like she wanted the truth more than she wanted to be protected."

"I guess you've gotten to know Willow pretty well during your time here."

"I think so. She's a special one, isn't she?"

"Yes," Theo said, trying without success to keep the emotion out of his voice. "She is."

"I'm going to miss how luxurious this place is, but I'm going to miss my conversations with her most of all. Don't let her get away."

"I think I already have."

"That's possible. We have to let people go when they need to leave. But I've seen how red her eyes are. I don't know if she'd have so many tears if she didn't still have some feelings for you."

His heart twisted itself into knots at the thought of Willow in tears. He wanted to take hope from Roni's words, but Willow had left him feeling certain that she didn't see a future for the two of them.

And even if there was some way that they could get back together, it wouldn't solve the other problem.

The fact was, that even though he'd made a terrible mistake, he had done it to protect Willow. And no matter what happened to change his role in Willow's life, he would always want to protect her. Whether he was her lover, friend, coworker… Even if he became nothing more to her than a distant memory, his first priority would always be her protection.

But Willow didn't want protection. She wanted honesty. How was he supposed to be honest if it hurt her?

And what if something serious did happen? This time, the biopsy had been clear. But what if the cancer came back? Or what if some other, unforeseen disaster befell them? Life was full of surprises, and not all of them were pleasant. He wanted to be someone who could offer Willow shelter, not someone who would add to her worries.

"Even if she does still feel something for me, it doesn't change that there's always the threat of something else looming over us. Cancer, or something else. Something even worse could go wrong."

"Now you're just being ridiculous."

He jerked back in surprise.

"Seriously. What you're saying is absurd. Unexpected problems can arise at any time. That's part of life, Doc. You of all people should know that, both as a doctor and as a cancer survivor. You sound like someone who's just trying to protect yourself from getting hurt."

Her words reminded him so much of what Becca had said, what Willow had said. He thought for a moment, trying to explain how he felt. He looked at the little dog, Buttons, nuzzled close at Roni's side. "Don't you ever worry about what would happen to Buttons if you couldn't take care of him anymore? Wouldn't you do anything to protect him, even if it meant giving him up?"

"Well. You're asking a billionaire with a full-time house staff, so take my answer with a grain of salt. I know that Buttons would be well cared for if anything happened to me. But even I didn't… I could never pass up the chance to have Buttons in my life, even if I didn't have two pennies to rub together. He's been such a comfort to me. And I would rather focus on enjoying the dogs—and the people—

who are in my life now, rather than worrying about what might happen later."

He said, a little sheepishly, "I've wanted a dog for a long time, but with the cancer... I was always worried about what would become of it if I couldn't take care of it anymore."

"That's your problem, if you don't mind me saying so, Doc. If you spend your life waiting until it's all smooth sailing, then you'll never get anything you want. You've got to grab your life with both hands and make the future you want for yourself. Cancer be damned. Change is going to happen no matter what. You might as well enjoy yourself while you can."

"But what if someone gets hurt? I just wanted to keep Willow from feeling any sadness. What if I just end up causing her more pain?"

"I don't know. But it seems like you're unilaterally deciding for yourself who should or shouldn't have to feel anything. Maybe she should be part of that decision, too."

He knew Roni was right. Once again, he could feel a dream slipping away from him. Years ago, he'd had the same feeling when he'd been told that he might not be able to have children. He'd done something about that, even though he'd known that freezing his sperm wasn't a guarantee that he'd have children someday. But it had brought him peace of mind, knowing that the option was there. And then Maisie had happened, not so much an accident, but a miracle in his opinion.

But this time, it was Willow who was slipping away, and the dreams he'd already begun for their life together. He'd known her for such a short time that he hadn't realized just how powerful those dreams had become. He hadn't even noticed, until now when he was faced with losing her, that every vision of the future he had included her. And yet now that dream was ending almost as soon as it had begun, and this time it wasn't the fault of some outside force. He couldn't blame this on the cancer. He realized now that the situation was entirely his fault, because of the choice he'd made to withhold information from Willow.

He'd been so stupid, he thought. He could have prevented all of this, if only he been paying attention. Willow had told him what she wanted. Even Becca had tried to warn him that he was making a mistake. And he could see now what he could have done differently, but he was very afraid that Willow had been right when she'd said it was too late.

Willow watched Theo and Roni from the hallway. She couldn't hear their conversation, but she could see Roni's smiles. Theo was so good with patients. There was something about his warm presence that they responded to immediately. She certainly knew how it felt to experience Theo's calm, earnest demeanor. Regardless of the difficulties that had arisen between them, no one could deny that Theo had a sincere desire to help his patients. Willow had always been impressed at how Theo approached each patient with exactly the same warmth. He was the same person with billionaire Roni Santiago that he was with any patient from St. Victoria. It was one of the things she had liked best about him.

It was still a trait that she appreciated, which was probably a good thing. She was glad she could still like Theo as a doctor, if not as a person.

She could see that he was a good doctor, a good man. Seeing the way he worked with cancer patients had shown her just how well Theo understood the fear and anxiety that came with a life-threatening illness. Her heart still ached for all he'd been through. And a part of her wanted, more than anything, to throw her arms around him and tell him that her feelings hadn't changed. But she couldn't trust that part of her. It might be nice, for a brief moment, to fantasize about holding Theo and telling him that they could have a future, and whatever that future brought, they'd face it together. But that fantasy would never come true, because Theo wasn't the kind of person who wanted to face things together. He'd shown her that clearly enough.

It had been very difficult to go into work each day. So difficult that she'd decided to take a few personal days, just to clear her head. She was glad she'd taken the time off. It had given her the space she needed to gain some clarity about what to do next.

At first, continuing to work in the same place as Theo had seemed impossible. How could she possibly stand seeing him every day? She'd thought briefly about leaving the Island Clinic and taking a job at St. Victoria Hospital. The pay would be far lower, but that might be less painful than seeing Theo.

She'd also considered asking Theo to leave, but that didn't seem fair. He'd come to St. Victoria to meet his daughter. He'd fulfilled every condition she'd set forth, and more. Their time together had simply been an unexpected diversion. He was a good doctor, and he cared deeply for Maisie. St. Victoria and the Island Clinic needed him. And Maisie needed him. She'd decided she couldn't deprive her daughter of the chance to feel connected to an extended family. No matter how heartbroken Willow might be, Maisie deserved to have the family support that Willow had always dreamed of.

She waited for Theo to finish up with Roni. As he turned away from Roni's bedside, she saw his face light up in recognition as he saw her standing in the shadows of the hallway. She noticed that it still hurt to see the way the corners of his mouth tugged up, as though his default expression were to smile. Dammit, she thought. It has to stop hurting someday. She just wished she knew when.

She motioned to him to step out into the hall with her, and they found a secluded corner.

"I'm so glad to see you," he said. "Are you here for a shift?"

"No," she said. "I'll come back officially tomorrow. But I'm here now to see you. I thought it would be good for the two of us to have a chance to talk, face-to-face, before I start again. So that we're both clear on where we stand with one another."

"Please," he said. "Can't I just have one more chance to explain?"

She closed her eyes. She knew she shouldn't listen. But she couldn't bring herself to stop him, either. She wished there were something, anything, that he could say that could make everything better.

"I don't want to let this go. To let *us* go," he said. "There has to be some way to fix it."

"I wish there were."

"You were right, you know. When you said that this is something I do. I do push people away. Usually the people I care about most. Part of it's because my family is so close-knit. I love that, but I love having privacy, too. And when my dad was diagnosed with Alzheimer's, it almost broke me to see all the pain they were going through. I couldn't stand the thought of adding to it."

He took her hand. "And then you became someone who was close to me, too. And when I think of the pain my family went through... I knew that I never wanted to put anyone I cared about through something like that. Not if I could help it. And so I was desperate to spare you.

"But I know that wasn't right. You didn't want to be spared the truth. I should have told you, right away, what was going on. I should never have tried to hide anything from you. Please, I'd do anything to have another chance. To show you I've changed."

She took her hand back. "No. I think we're just going to go around in circles." The words were hard to say, but it would have been harder still to have left them unsaid.

He took a long, slow breath. The look on his face cut her to the core. Then he said, "So what do we do now?"

"Well. That's what I came here to talk to you about."

It was as though a light had dimmed from his eyes. She could see that it was painful for him to speak. But better that they were having this conversation now, rather than later.

"Under other circumstances, I might offer to leave," he said. "I hate the idea of you feeling uncomfortable when we see each other here at work, or anywhere on the island. My leaving would probably make everything less complicated for both of us."

The words sent a jolt through her. It was a possibility she'd considered, but to hear him say it out loud made it real. There was something almost *wrong* about those words.

But then he continued. "I can't, though. Even if you never want to see me again, I can't leave. If you don't want me to see Maisie, I'll understand. But I have to be here for her, in case she ever needs me."

"I know. You're right, you should stay." His eyes widened, and she clarified. "You can see Maisie. Your relationship with her shouldn't be contingent on what happens with us. I need a little more time to pass before I'm ready to set up anything regularly. I'm just…not ready for that conversation yet. But I wanted you to know that eventually we'll figure out some way for you to spend time with her."

The relief on his face was evident, and she felt another wave of warmth toward him. He cared so much for Maisie. But at this moment, warmth was not a helpful feeling. She needed to stay firm in her resolve.

"Getting to know you has been good for Maisie. I can see that. And I want her to know her extended family. I don't want anything that's happened to us to take that from her. And we've both always said that we didn't want her to get hurt as a result of our involvement with one another."

"Thank you, Willow. This means more to me than you can possibly imagine."

"As far as work goes, I know that you're usually at St. Victoria Hospital in the mornings. So I'll just stick to morning shifts, and I can't imagine we'll have to deal with one another too often." She couldn't believe the way her words were coming out: cool and professional. There was no hint of the emotions that had been roiling within her over the past few days. But then, perhaps it was simply because the heartbreak had pushed her to a place beyond feeling.

"I could leave the Island Clinic and get a job somewhere else," he offered.

"Where? You already tried St. Victoria Hospital, and they sent you here. There are no other medical centers on the island. Where else would you work?"

"I…don't have to be a doctor."

"Are you saying that because it's true, or because it's what you think I want to hear?"

"I'm saying it because I mean it. Because even though being an oncologist is important to me, your well-being is more important. And I'm saying it because even though you might be all right with the two of us working together, *I* don't know if I can handle it."

She gave him a watery smile. "Don't you dare decide you're quitting medicine. You've got research studies that are about to start at the hospital. People are counting on those for their care. You're a good doctor, Theo. And you've never had the chance to really shine in your career, due to circumstances outside of your control. But I know you could. And I know that the patients here need you. They need someone who understands the fear, who's been where they've been. You belong here."

Now it was her turn to reach out for his hand. Probably for the last time. "I hope you understand what I'm saying. That I can understand how much you want to be in Maisie's life, and that I think we can work together."

"And nothing more."

She steeled her resolve. She'd come this far, and if she gave in now, she'd never be able to get through this conversation again. "You've earned the right to be here. And to be in Maisie's life. But as far as I'm concerned, you and I are through."

CHAPTER TEN

Willow sat on her sofa at home, the soft patter of rain tapping out a comforting beat on her roof. She'd packed Maisie off to Mrs. Jean's for a few hours so that she could have some peace and quiet. Or at least some quiet. Peace had been hard to come by for the past several days.

It was one thing to know, in her head, that she and Theo were over. But her heart didn't seem to have caught up. Even though she'd only been with Theo for a short time, signs of him were everywhere. She had photos of him on their phone from hikes they'd taken together. There was a recipe for his great-aunt Myrtle's chile taped to the front of her refrigerator. A small vase he'd bought for her still rested on her kitchen countertop, a single lily protruding from its mouth. She hadn't been able to bring herself to put it away. It was amazing, she thought, how quickly the individual moments of a relationship turned into memories. Even after just a few weeks, there were so many objects strewn across the landscape of her life, each one bringing up a different memory, a different feeling.

It was hard, too, when Maisie asked to see him. Theo had made an impression on her child quickly. Certainly Theo was very good with children, but Willow wondered if it wasn't so much about Theo's skill as something Maisie needed. Hard as it was to admit, Maisie was growing up. The swimming lessons that had once been a source of anxiety were now simply part of everyday life. Willow loved to see Maisie growing more confident in the water, but there was an ache, too, when she thought about how her child was growing a little taller and a little more independent every day. She needed more than just Willow in her life.

Willow knew that someday soon she would need to find a way to explain to Maisie who Theo was to her. She wished that Gran could be around for that conversation. It wasn't that she had any trepidation about raising the topic with Maisie. She knew that, ultimately, her child would simply understand that she was loved. But Gran always had such a precise way of putting things. She could always find the right words for any situation.

She often found herself missing Gran the

most on rainy days. Gran had loved the rain. She'd found it soothing. But then, Gran had never given the appearance of needing much soothing. She'd been a tough, independent woman who never seemed ruffled, even when times were hard.

Willow wondered how Gran had done it all. She'd held down a job as a librarian, raised a daughter and lost her own husband, Willow's grandfather, many years ago. And then, just as she was planning to retire, Willow's parents had passed away, and Gran was left to raise Willow on her own. She must have known moments of loneliness and frustration, but Willow could not recall a moment when her grandmother hadn't been cheerful and loving. Gran had done it all on her own, without ever needing help from anyone else.

And if Gran could do it, then so could she.

She'd been so right to swear off relationships. She'd given romance a chance, and look what had happened. Days spent wallowing in heartbreak, time taken off work to recover and now the extra unwanted emotional turmoil she had to deal with every time she saw Theo at the clinic. Giving in to her attraction to Theo had completely disrupted her life. And she didn't have time for disruption. She was a single mother. She had responsibilities. She recalled that Gran had never once dated for as long as Willow had known her. Gran had understood that being a mother meant that one couldn't afford certain kinds of complications in life.

Willow was certain that Gran wouldn't have faulted her for her decision to date Theo…but she probably wouldn't have made the same decision herself. Gran was far too responsible for boyfriends. *That's where I went wrong*, Willow thought. The whole time she'd been raising Maisie, she'd been trying to follow Gran's example. She should never have strayed. She should have given Theo a firm, decisive "No" the first time he'd asked her out, and thought nothing more of it.

Willow pulled out an old photo album and flipped through the pages. Here were memories of birthday parties and holidays. There were a few with Gran and Maisie, right after Maisie was born. But most were pictures of Willow's childhood.

It surprised her how many were of her and Gran alone. That was only natural, of course. It wasn't as though there had been other relatives to be part of things.

She traced one of her favorite photos with her finger. It was one of the few pictures of herself and her parents, with Gran in the background, from when she was very small. Underneath, in Gran's spidery handwriting, was the caption "The whole family together."

The words gave Willow a pang. The whole family indeed. She'd always thought that she and Maisie were doing just fine on their own. But that didn't mean that she didn't want more for both of them.

And now her family was small again. Just her and Maisie. But Maisie would have more, through Theo, and that was the important thing.

As she put the photo album back on the shelf, a stray picture fell out. She bent down to retrieve it and realized it was one she hadn't seen before. It must have been stuck behind one of the other photos.

It took her a moment to understand what she was seeing. And as she did, she could understand why she'd never seen the photo before.

It was a picture of Gran. Based on how she looked, Willow estimated that it would have been taken around the time Willow was in middle school or high school. But in the picture, Gran was at a party.

Which was odd. Willow didn't remember Gran ever going to parties. But then, Willow supposed she'd never wondered much about what Gran got up to when Willow was watched by a babysitter, or sleeping over at a friend's house, or at a party of her own. She'd always assumed that Gran was visiting antique markets with her friends, or baking another one of her prize-winning pies, or sitting demurely at home, perhaps...knitting?

In this photo, she was not baking, or knitting, or doing any of the things Willow typically thought of as Gran-like activities.

In this photo, a man was kissing Gran. And she was kissing him right back.

And the man's hands weren't chastely at his sides. One was around Gran's waist. The other...well, Willow could see why Gran might have tucked the photo quietly behind one of the more family-friendly pictures in the album.

She turned the photo over in confusion. To her surprise, Gran had dated the photo in the corner. It must have been important to her; Gran only dated the important ones. And a tiny, neat inscription was at the bottom.

Weekly supper party with Naveen. A tender lover and a better friend. It is love that makes the impossible possible.

A tender *lover*?
Had Gran had a boyfriend?

She turned the photo over and over, as though doing so would somehow give her more information. But the photo remained as much of a mystery as ever.

Or at least, it remained a mystery as long as she ignored the obvious, which was that Gran had had a boyfriend. In fact, judging by the dress Gran was wearing and the people at the party in that photograph, Gran had had an entire life that Willow had known nothing about. A life that didn't seem to focus much on knitting and baking.

It had simply never occurred to Willow to think about Gran's love life. Her grandfather had passed away long before Willow was born, and Gran had kept his picture on the mantel and spoken fondly of him from time to time. As a teenager, Willow had gone through a romantic phase where she'd invented a tragic love story between her grandparents. She believed that Gran, having suffered such a loss, was unwilling to take a chance on love again. She'd told the story to Gran, who had laughed and assured her that her time with Willow's grandfather was a treasured memory, but not a source of constant grief. Still, Willow's adolescent mind had been entranced with the idea of Gran as an epic heroine who'd lost her greatest love too early in life.

As an adult, especially after single motherhood, Willow's assumptions had taken a more practical turn. Gran, she thought, had probably been far too busy with childrearing and work responsibilities to have any time for romance. And Gran's interests had always seemed so innocent. She'd loved trying new recipes and new sewing patterns. True, she occasionally brought friends over to their small London flat, and some of those friends had been men...but it had never occurred to Willow that Gran might have been dating some of those men.

She squinted again at the picture of Naveen and realized that he looked a little familiar. She couldn't recall much, but she was absolutely certain that he was one of the "friends" that had come over to Gran's small flat for occasional drinks and conversation.

She shook her head in amazement. *Gran's boyfriend.* She was surprised to find that it made her happy to think of Gran dating. She'd always thought Gran had given up things like dating and parties in order to take care of Willow. But judging by the photograph, Gran hadn't given up those things entirely.

It seemed she'd found a way to fit them into her life, after all.

She thought about the quote Gran had included.

It is love that makes the impossible possible.

Had Gran been in love with this Naveen, then? He was certainly handsome-looking in the photograph. She wished so much that Gran were here so they could talk about it now. There was an entire side of Gran's life that she'd known nothing about.

What would Gran think about what had happened with Theo? Just a moment ago, she'd been worrying that Gran might have disapproved of her choice to date Theo in the first place. But now that she'd seen that photograph, she wondered if Gran might have an entirely different perspective.

As shocked as she was about the idea of Gran having a boyfriend, the more Willow thought about it, the more it made sense. Gran was the kind of woman who'd always invited love into her life. It was stranger to think of her never having a boyfriend.

Gran would probably not have approved of Theo's tendency to avoid pain for himself and others by cutting himself off from everyone. But she might also have suggested that Willow was doing the same thing. By swearing off relationships, she'd been trying to protect herself from all of the pain and turmoil she believed they caused. She'd been trying to avoid all the hurt she'd felt with Jamie.

In other words, she'd been scared. But what if there was no sure way to protect herself from being hurt? What if, rather than protecting herself, she was simply cutting herself off from love?

She'd always believed that Gran had lived her life without love and had gotten by just fine. But now it seemed she'd been wrong about that. Gran hadn't sworn off relationships, she'd just been discreet about them. Willow would give anything for a chance to ask Gran about what had happened with Naveen. But whether Gran had found love or not, she'd clearly been willing to give it a chance. Quite an enthusiastic chance, given how things appeared in the photograph.

Could she say the same for herself? For the first time since meeting Theo—in fact, for the first time in the past few years—Willow realized that she couldn't. Fear, plain and simple, had been holding her back. And that wasn't Theo's fault. In a way, it wasn't even Jamie's fault. Jamie had hurt her, yes. He'd left her feeling deeply betrayed. But she was the one who'd let fear get in the way of opening her heart to the possibility of the one thing she desired most in the world. She was so afraid of losing love. But if she couldn't be open to it in the first place, then she'd never be able to have the family she'd spent her life dreaming of.

It had been right there in front of her. Theo was Maisie's father. And she loved him. She knew that now. The idea of depending on someone, *needing* someone, scared her so much. But the idea of being closed off scared her even more. She'd accused Theo of being unable to access his emotions, but wasn't she just as guilty? She'd convinced herself that she was too busy for love, that relationships could only lead to heartbreak, that she'd get hurt again, the same way she'd been before. But the whole time, she'd just been letting her fear get the best of her. And she'd almost lost what was most important to her.

These past few days without Theo had been nearly unbearable. But not as unbearable as the thought that she might have lost him entirely. She grabbed her car keys from the counter. She had to talk to Theo, had to tell him exactly how she felt, no matter how he reacted. She desperately wanted to give him her heart, but she couldn't imagine what he might do with it.

She might be afraid to give him her heart, but she could give him something else: a chance. Because she loved him. And love deserved another chance.

She'd barely left her front door when she stopped short. Theo was standing in front of her, rain pouring down his face.

"I hope you don't mind that I came over," he said. "I've been trying to give you your space. But I had something I wanted to show you."

"Theo, I need to tell you something."

"Just wait. Please. I'd like to bring you over to my place and show you something. Don't say anything until then. It's just a short drive. Please."

She wanted to explain, to tell him all she felt and hope that they could both give things another chance. But Theo was so insistent.

They made the short drive to his house, and both stepped out of the car.

"Here it is," Theo said.

Willow was confused. "I've seen your house before, Theo."

"Keep looking. Notice anything different about the porch?"

There it was. The dog bed and toys were gone. "What's happened to Bixby?"

Theo stepped forward and opened the door. "He lives inside now."

Willow's face was starting to become very wet. The rain, of course. It was pattering down steadily. Surely it was the rain that collected in the corners of her eyes.

"You've finally let him in."

"It was time. It should have been done long ago. I should have started letting a lot of people in, long ago."

She couldn't help smiling at him then, though her tears were flowing freely. "Sometimes it just takes practice."

"There's something else I want to show you, as well. Come onto the porch, so you don't get wet."

She stepped onto the porch, and he took out his phone. "Look at your phone, too," he said. "Open your calendar."

She pulled out her phone and looked at the calendar. There were dozens and dozens of appointment invitations awaiting her response. Medical appointments.

"This shows every one of the follow-up appointments I have scheduled so far," he said. "I'm afraid there's quite a lot of them. You know how particular oncologists can be. My medical team insists that I attend numerous checkups to track how my remission is going.

And I want you to attend every single one of them with me. I want the person who matters to me most to be there. I want someone who loves and supports me to be at my side, and it would mean everything to me for you to be that person."

She tried to respond, but she couldn't quite speak, whether it was because of her laughter or her tears.

"I want you with me," Theo continued. "I want you to be there because no matter what the future holds, I don't want to go through it alone. I want all three of us to go through it together, as a family. And I want to be a proper father for Maisie. For three years, I was so focused on trying to protect her that I couldn't even be there for her in the first place. But I'm ready to be here for her now. And I'm not afraid of what might happen, because no matter what's in store for us, we can choose to go through it together. And if you'll have me, Willow, then I want to go through it with you. I'll give you my whole self. The good, the bad and everything in between. That is, if it's something you still want. If *I'm* someone you still want. Because I love you. I love you more than I ever thought it was possible to love. I want us to be a family together. But there's one thing I want even more than that."

"What?" she said, breathless, still trying to take it all in.

"I want you to love me back."

A moment later, she was in his arms, his kiss crushing her lips and sending shivers down her spine. She tried to put everything she was feeling into the kiss. It was a kiss that held more than three long years of waiting, her hopes and wishes for the future and all her love for him.

It was the kind of kiss, she thought, that might have made a woman like Gran raise an appreciative eyebrow.

After a long moment, they broke apart, and Theo said, "I don't want to get my hopes up too much. But this seems like a fairly enthusiastic response to my invitation to attend all of my medical appointments."

She reached up to put her arms around his neck and leaned against him. "Some girls get flowers along with declarations of love. I get to be included in your medical appointments. And that's exactly what I want. Because I love you, too, Theo."

"Do you?" he said, his forehead pressed against hers. "Because I was worried that I had ruined everything."

"You weren't the only one who made mistakes. Or the only one who has a hard time being emotionally vulnerable. I accused you of holding back when I was doing exactly the same thing—looking for ways to convince myself that I didn't have room for love in my life, looking for proof that I was right not to trust. I was trying so hard to protect what I had that I didn't even realize what I was missing."

"And what was that exactly?"

She kept her arms around his neck, pulling herself close to him. "A chance to have the family I've always wanted. And a chance to have it with *you*."

He kissed her again, lightly, and before he pulled away, she let her lips brush the corner of his mouth, just where it seemed to curve up into a smile. There was a long silence then, as they held each other and exchanged soft, slow kisses, while the rain continued to pour down just beyond the porch.

After quite some time had passed, Willow spared a quick glance at the calendar on her phone. "This is a lot of appointments."

"Don't I know it. The first year is the worst as far as follow-up goes. They want to do examinations often to keep an eye on things. But then after the first year they start to lighten up a bit, and once you get a few years out it's just once in a while. The five-year appointment is the big one. If you're still in complete remission by then, you're declared cured."

"Five years is a long time." She looked into his eyes, the question left unspoken between them. "It's certainly a long time to be in each other's lives."

He pulled her close. "In a way, we've already been in each other's lives for a long time, because of Maisie. I stupidly thought the best thing I could do for both of you was to stay away, so as not to add any pain to your lives. But now I realize that I shouldn't have just stopped at touching your life. I should have reached out and grabbed on with both hands."

"I'm so glad you finally are."

"This time, I'm not letting go. Because I think the more we reach for one another, the better things will get. I might be wrong, but that's what I believe. Do you want to stay together and see if I'm right?"

"I do."

EPILOGUE

Six months later

"MOMMY, LOOK! I can hold Daddy's laptop and my grape juice *and* three books all at the same time!"

Willow raced into Theo's dining room to assess the situation. Maisie loved to explore more than ever, and her adventures often included tests of her own capabilities that frequently ended in disaster, whether in the form of broken items or bumps and bruises. And now that they were spending so much time at Theo's house, there were even more new things to discover—and, potentially, to break.

Willow was just in time to rescue Theo's laptop as it was about to slip out of Maisie's hands. The little girl had three books tucked under her chin, and was trying to hold on to a cup of grape juice and Bixby's collar in the other.

"Okay, let's not dye Bixby purple," she said, freeing the dog from Maisie's grasp.

"It might be too late for that," said Theo, deftly taking the laptop from her. "I think she got a little on one of his back legs earlier."

"Guess it can't be helped. At least one of us will look distinctive." She started to comb Maisie's hair, but then caught a look at herself in the dining room mirror and began to brush furiously at her own hair instead. "How many minutes until showtime?"

Theo slipped an arm around her waist. "Just a few, but it won't be the end of the world if we're a little late. You're not nervous, are you?"

She hesitated. "I just wish I'd had a little more time to spend on Maisie's hair this morning. And mine's so frizzy in this humidity. I want to make a good first impression."

"Are you kidding? They're going to love you as much as I do. Well, *almost* as much as I do. And it's not really your first impression. You and Becca never seem to get off the phone with one another. I can barely get a conversation in with her anymore because she's always talking to you."

"But I haven't met the rest of them. And I haven't seen *any* of them face-to-face." She looked at the laptop. "Such as it is."

"Face to laptop. Hey." He pulled her close.

"You look absolutely beautiful. And if by some bizarre fluke my family is not completely smitten with you, well...they're four thousand miles away. They can't do much to you from that distance."

Willow called Maisie to her, and the three of them sat in front of the computer monitor as Theo flicked it on. A moment later, Theo's family appeared on-screen.

There was a cavalcade of aunts, uncles and cousins. Willow had got on well with Theo's sister, Becca, but he had three other siblings who were delighted to meet her, as well. Everyone seemed to adore Maisie, who could barely contain her glee as she saw young cousins her own age.

Theo's father was there, as well, seated next to Theo's mother, and surrounded by his own siblings. Though he clearly benefited from the support of those around him, his father appeared to be in good spirits. Willow noticed how tender Theo's mother's expression was as she sat beside him, and she had a feeling that their years together had been happy.

As far as Willow could tell, there were three, possibly four, generations of family in one room. She'd never seen anything like it. Everyone talked at once, but somehow it seemed to work. Willow could imagine what it might be like to be in the room with these people: everyone talking over each other, full of energy and excitement. Everyone seemed to have a family story to share, but they made certain that Willow was included, too. Theo was able to tell his family that he was now in complete remission, with no detectable amount of cancer in his body, and cheers went up in London and the Caribbean.

It was getting to be evening by the time they ended the call. As Theo switched off the computer, Willow quickly wiped a tear from her eye.

"What's this?" he said. "You did great. They absolutely loved you, just as I knew they would. And it seemed as though you were having a good time, too."

"I was. I loved meeting them, all of them. Becca's even funnier in person. And your mother was so warm and kind. It was wonderful."

"Then why the tears?"

"I've always wanted a family like that. Growing up, it did get lonely at times, with just me and Gran. I'm so glad to see that Maisie gets to have so much family in her life."

"Willow." Theo pulled her up from her chair and put his hands around her shoulders.

"They're not just Maisie's family. They're going to be your family, too."

He pulled a small box from the mantelpiece behind them. Willow hadn't noticed it before, but as she saw it in Theo's hands, her heart began to race.

Theo knelt down. "Willow Thompson," he began.

"Yes!" she cried, and threw her arms around him. He stood up and kissed her.

"There's something you need to know about this ring," he said.

Willow gently traced her finger over the ring's intricate setting. "The filigree is so detailed, this must be an antique."

"Yes. It belonged to my grandmother. At first, I was planning to look for something new. But the more I thought about it, I realized that I wanted to propose with my grandmother's ring. I talked it over with her, and with all my siblings and cousins who aren't married yet, and they all agreed with me that you should be the one to have it. Assuming you like it, of course."

"Oh, Theo. It's beautiful."

"This isn't just about the two of us, my love. I wanted you to have something that would show you, every day, that you're joining a huge family you'll be part of forever, no matter what happens to me. I want this ring to be a reminder that our family will be more than just the three of us."

"Well. I already knew it would be more than just the three of us."

He stared at her, stunned. "Willow. Have you been keeping a secret from me?"

She smiled. "I suppose it's time you knew. I'm pregnant."

Unmitigated joy broke over his face. He pressed his forehead against hers, and pulled her close to him. "Who would have thought that I'd get a second chance at having everything I wanted," he said.

"I'm so glad you're happy."

"Are you joking? I'm thrilled. How could you imagine I'd feel any other way?"

"Well, you know. Unexpected surprises aren't always easy to deal with."

He buried his nose in her hair. "Thank goodness for unexpected surprises," he murmured. "This time, I'm going to be there for everything, no matter what might come our way."

* * * * *

*If you missed the previous story in the
The Island Clinic quartet, then check out*

How to Win the Surgeon's Heart
by Tina Beckett

*And there are two more tropical
stories to come
Available August 2021!*

*Also, if you enjoyed this story, check out
these other great reads from Julie Danvers*

Falling Again in El Salvador
From Hawaii to Forever

All available now!